A
Bridge Reader

A FELLHOUNDS OF THESK STORY

MOON CHASE

by

Cathy Farr

Llyfrgelloedd Caerdydd
www.caerdydd.gov.uk/llyfrgelloedd
Cardiff Libraries
www.cardiff.gov.uk/libraries

CAERDYDD
CARDIFF

BiTE
Publishing

Cathy Farr is hereby identified as the author of this work in accordance with section 77 of the Copyright, Design and Patents Act 1988

This book is published by BITE Publishing, Cardiff.

A copy of this book is available at
the National Library of Wales and the British Library.
ISBN 978-0-9928509-0-6

The book cover pictures are copyright to
Sam Wall (samwall.com)
Illustrations within the book are copyright to
Alan Marks (marksonpaper.co.uk)
Map of Thesk is copyright to Cathy Farr
Design and typesetting by Ritchie Craven.
Printed in Wales, UK by Gomer Press (gomerprinting.co.uk)

About
Bridge Readers™

Designed by BITE Publishing, Bridge Readers© help improving readers to develop their reading skills as they move towards Young Adult and Adult fiction.

Ideal for weaker and improving readers, reluctant readers and those learning English as a second language.
They contain no bad language or sexual content
– they're just really great reads.

Bridge Readers™
bridging the gap between learning to read
and reading to learn

Author Notes

Cathy Farr fell in love with Irish wolfhounds as a teenager but she had to wait over twenty years to own one. The original Young Adult edition of *Moon Chase* was inspired by Cathy's first wolfhound, Finn. Irish wolfhound's stand at eye level with most children and it was their reaction to Cathy's own giant hound that gave her the idea for the Fellhounds of her stories. Cathy has written short pieces for BBC Radio Wales and press articles; she once re-wrote an article by her boss that nearly got her sacked!

Cathy adapted *Moon Chase* as a **Bridge Reader** after working with ESL and SLCN children in local schools and with the charity Afasic Cymru*. *Moon Chase* (the original) was Cathy's first novel, published in 2010; *Moon Crossing,* the second in the YA series, will soon be available as a **Bridge Reader**, too.

*Afasic is a parent led organisation representing children and young people with specific language impairment (SLI) and speech, language and communication needs (SLCN); their work has helped open the world of words to many who would otherwise still find that door firmly closed. To find out more about SLCN and Afasic's work, visit www.afasiccymru.org.uk or www.afasic.org.uk

For Finn

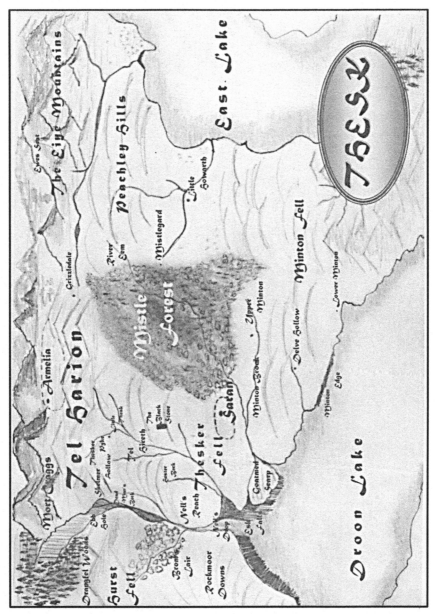

CHAPTER ONE

Unfriendly Visitors

It was a misty morning. The boy blew onto his cupped hands to keep them warm. Above him he could see two silvery half-moons in the dawn sky. It was his favourite time of day on Thesker Fell – too early for the midges that would bite him later and make him itch; and too light for the eagards – huge birds of prey that hunted during the night.

The boy studied the vast hills in front of him. It had been a very hot summer and the sun had dried out the grass, turning it brown and orange. He knew it would take more than one shower of rain to make it green again. The boy was not alone though. A herd of young deer munched on the grass at the edge of a nearby forest; and a huge, shaggy hound sat next to him sniffing the dawn air and watching the young animals.

'Only one more day to go, Farrow, and then we can go home,' said the boy, cutting into a huge wedge[1*] of cheese that he got from his bag. There was also a large, once fresh, loaf. But it had gone mouldy so he

* When you see a tiny number like this [1] take a look in the back of this book

1

wrinkled his nose and threw the bread high into the air where a huge black raven swooped down, grabbed it in its beak and flew off into the trees.

The boy bit into the cheese and stroked the hound's soft coat.

'Well, it's only one more day, old girl. One more day... but I bet Mr Mortens'll still be angry at me when we get home!'

Farrow put her huge head in the boy's lap. He gently curled her soft, velvety ear in his fingers and frowned.

'I mean, it wasn't as if – '

But he suddenly stopped talking.

Farrow sat up. Her head was much higher than the boy's and towering over him, she stared into the mist and pricked her ears[2] to listen. Seth swallowed his cheese in one gulp.

'What is it, girl?' he whispered and slowly reached for his crossbow. He listened but he couldn't hear a thing – not even the munching of the deer. Something was wrong. But just as he picked up his crossbow something flew through the air and hit him on the head, knocking him out. At that same moment, four men charged out of the forest. One was putting a stone into a sling-shot, two others carried vicious-looking swords and another waved a huge axe. All four men ran towards the boy.

But with a powerful spring, Farrow bounded straight into the men. She knocked three of them down a steep slope away from her master but unfortunately she missed the man holding the sling-shot. He aimed at her again. But before he could shoot, Farrow jumped at him, knocking him into the air. He landed with a loud *SNAP!* and lay on the ground with his head twisted around at a strange angle. He was dead.

Then Farrow saw one of the other men climbing back up the slope. But the sunlight reflected off his sword and she couldn't see. So she closed her eyes, sniffed and charged towards the smell of his sweat. He cried out. When she let go of his dead body, his blood dripped through her teeth onto the grass.

But there was no time to rest. More men had arrived. They were rushing to herd the deer into the forest but there were too many men for Farrow to fight on her own. Then Farrow saw the two surviving attackers. They were dragging her master's body towards the forest – he was still unconscious. Farrow let out a blood-curdling howl and galloped towards them. The men dropped the boy and pelted towards the trees. Farrow blocked their way and snarled. But one of the men lifted his sword over his head and charged. The blade cut into Farrow's shoulder. She howled in pain and anger. The man lashed at her again but this time he missed. Farrow sprang forward. She closed her huge jaws around his throat and lay on top of him, waiting until she had crushed his life from him.

There was only one man left. He was very close to the injured boy. Farrow knew her master was in terrible danger.

Man and hound stood watching each other for a moment. Then suddenly the man let out a mad laugh and charged towards the boy once again holding his axe above his head. Farrow sped[3] forward with her head low. She got there just in time. The axe fell. It sliced through her right ear, bounced off her iron collar and hit the ground with a loud thud. Quick as a flash[4] Farrow snapped her immense jaws shut – the man's headless body collapsed to the ground. Farrow swallowed.

Blood trickled down her leg from the deep slash on her shoulder. But Farrow was too worried about the boy to notice her own injuries. She whimpered quietly and licked the boy's face. She gently nuzzled her nose into his neck but he didn't move. He had a deep cut on his temple. It was bleeding badly and the grass underneath his head was red with his blood.

Farrow tried to make him wake up. She barked loudly. Then she tugged at his tunic. She even tried to drag him by his collar. But the fabric tore and she fell backwards with the cloth hanging in her clenched teeth.

The great hound sat down. She sniffed the air. Then, like an arrow, she ran towards the forest. She skidded to a halt at the edge of the dark woods and looked over her shoulder in case the boy called her back – but he didn't. She let out a sad howl. Then, with one more look back, she went into the dark forest.

She bounded through the trees, stopping every now and again to sniff the damp air. Then she sped on.

A rabbit suddenly sprang out of the darkness. It was startled by Farrow's sudden arrival but she did not chase it. She galloped on. There was a steep waterfall up ahead. She stopped, went back four steps and then turned around and ran. She jumped over the swirling water in one huge bound.

A long time later she came to a bright clearing in the trees. *SWOOSH!* She was caught in a huge net and hauled high into the air, swinging between two pine trees.

She was angry and scared, and she barked and barked. But the ropes got tighter when she struggled and made the cuts from the battle even worse. She was very tired now and her injuries hurt. There was no way out. So she lay still and began to howl.

CHAPTER TWO

Running into Trouble

Wil Calloway woke up suddenly and lay on his bed breathing heavily. He had been dreaming about the forest... and a *massive* dog. The dog had been fighting and there was a lot of blood... and howling. Wil sat up and wiped the sweat from his forehead. But he could still hear the dog. It was howling just as it had been in his dream. He rubbed his eyes to make sure he was awake. He shook his head and banged his ear but the terrible noise didn't go away.

He got out of bed and walked into the tiny round living room of his mother's house. His breakfast was on the table but he couldn't see his mother. Then he remembered; she was going to Upper Minton early this morning to sell some chickens.

Wil yawned and stretched. He walked out of the little cottage into the bright, sunny morning. No, he really *could* hear an animal howling, and by the look of it so could the whole village! Wil ran to the water barrel outside the front door and quickly splashed a handful of water over his face. The water was freezing. Now he really was awake.

Wil looked around. He could see that people had stopped what they were doing. Everyone was running towards the noise – and everyone looked frightened. Wil rushed back into his house. He grabbed his sword and pulled on his old boots. Then he raced back out and followed the people.

'It's a Fellhound,' yelled a villager who was further ahead. 'From up on Thesker Fell.'

A tall man carrying a big stick stretched his thin neck to get a better view over the crowd.

'I can't see anyone with it – maybe it's lost? Thesker Fell is a very long way from here!'

'Maybe his master's been killed!' said a tiny woman. She was clutching a frying pan in her fist. 'Lord Rexmoore's men have been around here again. Up to no good[5], I'll bet.'

'Someone told me Fellhounds can be vicious if they haven't got a master. Just kill it! At least it'll stop that racket,' shouted someone else.

By now a very big crowd had gathered. Men, women and children had all come to see what was making such a terrible noise.

Wil was taller than a lot of the other villagers. He pushed his way towards the front. Just as Wil got close to the man with the stick three people marched through the crowd. A loud voice spoke from behind them.

'Make way for the Elders[6] of Mistlegard!'

People moved out of the way to let them pass but then stepped back again. They were frightened of Farrow but they were very interested to see what was going to happen next.

Everyone was pushing and shoving. Wil trod on a woman's toe and then his sword dug into a man's ribs. The woman glared at him and the man yelped. Wil smiled. 'Sorry,' he whispered and continued to make his way towards the clearing where he could see a massive, blood-soaked hound. It was the injured animal from his dream.

A tall man with a jagged scar across his right cheek raised his hand for silence and began speaking in a loud voice.

'As the Elders of Mistlegard, Garth Fengal, Madam Gaskhill and I can see that this beast is badly wounded. It is dangerous. As its master is not here we order that she must be killed. Where is the village slaughterer[7]?'

Some people in the crowd cheered in agreement and a voice at the back shouted, *'HENRY! I HOPE YOUR SPEAR'S SHARP!'*

Henry, the village slaughterer, barged through from the back. But as he got closer to the hound he slowed down. His face went very pale. He raised his spear above his head and kept walking. Farrow was now lying still and quiet. She was watching him.

Everyone else held their breath.

Wil couldn't think of anything else to do so he shouted.

'*WAIT!*'

He was very surprised because everyone turned to look at him. They were waiting for him to do something so he tried his best to look confident and pushed his way towards the Elders. Everyone watched.

'I know this hound,' said Wil loudly. Then he looked at the Elders and whispered so that only they could hear. 'Well, actually, your Worships, I don't really know her but I–,' he stopped and then said, 'I *think* I dreamt about her this morning.'

He remembered the horrible scenes from his dream – especially the one with the unconscious boy with his head bleeding.

'I think her master has been badly wounded. He's on Thesker Fell. I think she's come because she can't help him on her own... um... her name's Farrow, by the way.'

'Huh! How do *you* know this, Wil Calloway?' Madam Gaskhill demanded. Wil could tell that she did not believe him. 'Your dreams have been wrong before, boy! I remember when you told everyone that the village was going to be attacked by wild animals. My children still have nightmares!'

'I know, Ma'am,' said Wil. 'But look, one half of my dream is there.' He pointed to Farrow. 'This hound's name is Farrow and she has come for our help, I know she has.'

Wil stepped towards the hound. The crowd gasped. Farrow looked at Wil and whimpered. The picture of the injured boy came back into Wil's head.

Wil turned to the third Elder who had not yet spoken.

'Garth, please. Let me set her free. I promise that she won't hurt anyone. If she does... well, you can kill me after you've killed her!'

Garth looked surprised.

'Now Wil, I don't think we will need to do that! Your mother would never forgive me!' Then Garth turned to Madam Gaskhill. 'After all, Matilda, he was right about the sheep at East Lake – we could have lost a lot more without Wil's warning!'

Madam Gaskhill put her hands on her hips and opened her mouth to speak. But Wil spoke first, he just couldn't stop himself.

'Look, I'm sorry, Ma'am... and Sirs, but I don't think we've got time to talk about this. A boy will die if we don't help. This hound can take me to him, I know she can.'

He took another step towards Farrow. Garth looked at Wil, then at the hound, and then Wil again. A drop of dark blood dripped from the netting. Wil wanted to scream out, '*This is taking too long!*'

Garth spoke.

'Wil, I agree that the hound should be given a chance. But, I warn you, if she takes just one step towards the village I will kill her myself. Madam Gaskhill? ... Master Gerald? Do you agree?'

After another long silence Master Gerald said, 'I agree.'

Madam Gaskhill looked very surprised.

Gerald continued in a loud voice so that everyone in the crowd could hear.

'Wil is going to set the animal free. If it attacks anyone I will kill it!'

'Well,' said Madam Gaskhill. 'I certainly do *not* agree!' And she turned and marched away through the crowd. Garth and Master Gerald said nothing. Wil took one more step towards Farrow and slid his sword very slowly out of his belt.

'Stand back everyone,' he ordered as bravely as he could. He didn't really know how he was going to control Farrow but he took a deep breath and began to cut the ropes that were holding her. He could see the deep wound on her shoulder.

'Steady now,' he whispered, cutting the last two

ropes with one slice of his sharp blade.

Free at last, Farrow leapt to her feet and closed her jaws around Wil's arm. A woman screamed. Garth pulled his sword from his belt.

'It's Okay! I'm Okay!' Wil shouted. Yes, Farrow did have her huge mouth around his arm but she was holding him so gently he could hardly feel her teeth on his skin.

She started to walk backwards very slowly. She was trying to pull Wil towards the forest.

'I think she wants me to follow her,' Wil shouted. Garth and Gerald moved towards them with their swords held ready to strike.

Farrow let go of Wil's arm and galloped back towards the trees. But she stopped at the edge of the forest and turned back. She stood there panting and slowly wagging her long, powerful tail. Wil ran towards her.

'Wait, Wil! You can't go alone!' called Master Gerald. 'There are bears and wild boar in the forest! You've got to take someone with you.'

But with an impatient bark Farrow turned and disappeared into the trees. Wil knew there was no time to wait. So he tucked his sword back into his belt and ran.

'No time, Master Gerald,' he called over his shoulder. 'I don't think she'll wait! Tell my mother I'll be back soon... and tell her not to worry!'

CHAPTER THREE

Seeing is Believing

Wil tried to follow Farrow as she galloped through the thick forest. The further they went, the darker it got. He had been into Mistle Forest many times, but he had always kept close to the village – and, he remembered, he had *always* been with people armed with crossbows and spears!

Wil stopped. He had no idea where he was but Farrow cantered in a big circle around him and then ran off again into the dark trees.

In a very short time Wil started to get tired. He stopped again, panting. He couldn't see Farrow anywhere. Then he remembered Master Gerald's warning about bears and wild boar and decided that shouting might not be a good idea. So he stood and waited, hoping that Farrow would come back very soon. The forest was very quiet but the sound of fast-running water told him he was close to the River Eem with its high waterfalls and dangerous rapids.

A bush nearby suddenly shook. Wil reached for his sword. Farrow jumped out onto the path. She let out one very loud bark as if she was asking Wil why he was standing still. Then she bounded off again.

Wil ran on. But as he ran he started to worry. What if he was wrong? Maybe it was a trap?

Wil could hear the sound of a river flowing fast. It was in the direction that Farrow was leading him. He had no idea how they would get across but then he saw a fallen tree. Its huge trunk was making a very useful bridge and Farrow was already on the distant bank. She barked again.

The bark of the tree was wet and covered in thick, green moss. Wil clung on to the spiky branches to stop himself from falling into the water a long way below. When he reached the other side he was soaked through and covered in dark green slime.

But Farrow barked again – there was no time to dry off.

After a long time running, Wil finally reached the edge of the forest. He crouched down and blinked into the bright sunlight. After a moment he could see fields and hills, bushes and windswept trees. But he couldn't see Farrow. Salty sweat trickled into Wil's eyes and made them sting. It dripped off his nose onto his arm. He looked out at the hills. Maybe someone was waiting to attack him?

Wil started to get worried. Close by, half a dozen crows were pecking greedily at something red. Wil stared. What were they eating? Then he realised – it was one of the headless bodies from his dream. He looked away and tried not to be sick.

Then Wil saw Farrow. She was standing over a dark bundle – a very still, dark bundle. He stood up and ran as fast as he could towards the hound. Crows flew into the air as he ran past more dead bodies.

Wil reached the boy and carefully rolled him onto his back; it really was the boy from his dream. The boy moaned – he was alive! The grass was black with dried blood and Wil could see tiny little cuts on the boy's head where the crows had started to peck at his blood-soaked head.

Wil looked around and swore under his breath. In his rush to follow Farrow he hadn't thought to bring anything with him – not even a flask of water! He knelt on the ground next to the boy's bloody body. He was trying to think what to do next when something very hard hit him on the back of the head. Everything went black.

Wil woke with a gasp. Someone had just thrown ice-cold water over his face.

'Finally awake then?' a voice whispered into his ear. It was not a friendly voice.

A second voice spoke. This one sounded nervous and weak.

'I knew that would wake him up, Cedric.'

Wil blinked. His head pounded. He could see two of everything and when he moved his head the dizziness got worse. For the second time that day he had to try very hard not to be sick. It was only then he realised that his arms were tied behind his back.

'What the...?' Wil groaned and slumped back on the ground.

The men who had woken him were busy with the boy. He was still unconscious; Farrow was lying quietly next to him. Behind the men Wil could see two horses. They had saddles and bridles – all ready for a journey.

A rock was digging into Wil's back. How long had he been unconscious? Why he was tied up? Would he get the blame for the boy's injuries?

'How is he?' Wil called, trying to sound friendly. 'I got here as quickly as I could, but...'

'Silence, boy!' The man called Cedric shouted. He poured water onto a cloth and dabbed the deep cut on the boy's head. 'It's no use pretending. We know you did this! You and your dead friends! Five against one. Very brave. Lord Rexmoore would be proud of you!'

Wil really hoped he was still dreaming. He pinched himself. It hurt. He really was awake.

'I... I don't know what you mean? Those men weren't my friends. I don't know them!' he insisted. 'The hound came to my village to get help... I stopped the Elders from killing her. She brought me here. The men were dead already. I didn't kill anyone. *The boy had already been hurt!'*

Cedric stood up slowly. His white face looked worried. He turned and marched towards Wil. He didn't stop until his nose was almost touching Wil's. Wil could smell Cedric's horrible breath.

'I don't believe you!' the man growled. 'It's not enough that Rexmoore sends his bullies to our village to take our food to pay his taxes. Now he is sending his men into our fields to kill our children!'

'Really... No, I didn't! I wasn't with them. I hate Rexmoore. I didn't hurt the boy. I came to help.'

'*Lies!* We will take you to Lady Élanor. She will make you tell the truth. She will give you her truth potion. It works very well... but it might kill you!' Cedric walked away cackling[8]. Then, without turning around, he shouted, 'But if my son dies, I will kill you myself!'

Wil gritted his teeth and tried to stay calm. Why wouldn't they believe him? He took a deep breath and tried again.

'Look, I did not hurt your son. I came to help. Farrow led me here.'

The ropes were cutting into his wrists and his elbows ached where they were twisted behind his back.

The men ignored him.

Wil tried again.

'OK. If I *did* attack your son, why didn't his hound kill me like she killed the others? And why isn't there any blood on my sword?'

Cedric stopped what he was doing.

Wil waited. The older man stood up and looked at the hound. Then he pointed to Wil's sword lying on the ground near the remains of a tiny campfire.

'Arbert, fetch me that sword.'

Arbert did as he was told. He held out the sword with a shaking hand. Cedric took the blade looked at it carefully. He held it up to get a good look at its sharp edges in the sunlight. After a long time he spoke.

'Hm! You're right, boy. There's no blood on your sword... but maybe you hid in the trees until the fight was over?'

Cedric pressed the point of the sword into Wil's throat.

'Or *maybe*… she just left you until last?' And with a sudden, cruel laugh he plunged the weapon down into the ground between Wil's legs. Then he turned and walked back to his injured son, leaving Wil wondering if Cedric really had meant to miss.

Insects buzzed around Wil's head. He had been walking behind the horses for a very long time. He was dirty and very tired. The ropes, still tied around his wrists, cut into him with every step he took.

Cedric's son lay across the saddle of one of the horses. Arbert, also on foot leading the horse, was limping and sweaty. Cedric was riding the other horse, a fine animal that pranced[9] along, unhappy to be moving so slowly.

At the next corner Farrow suddenly galloped up a dusty track towards a pair of huge wooden gates. They were shut tight and when she discovered she could not go any further she barked – the same loud bark that Wil had heard in the forest. The sound echoed out across the Fells.

'Stop, who goes there?' shouted a voice from behind the gate.

'Eldridge, open the gate. Let us in and get Lady Élanor. Seth's been attacked up on Tel Hireth. Then,' Cedric shouted, looking at Wil, 'tell the Order we've got a prisoner!'

People came running down streets and out of houses. Wil heard the gates close with a soft bang behind him. He was now shut inside the village.

Arbert dropped his horse's reins and ran to a water-trough nearby. He dunked his whole head into the water, before scooping up handfuls which he drank noisily while water dripped off his wet head.

His horse went straight to the water, too, and as Wil was still tied to its saddle, he had no choice but to follow. But he didn't mind. He dipped his hot face into the cool water and drank huge gulps.

But Farrow didn't even try to drink; she dropped on the ground in the shade with her long back against the cold stone. She had used every last bit of energy getting home.

All around people were shouting. A young girl appeared out of a narrow alley, her long, silver hair flowing behind her as she ran towards them. She went straight to the unconscious boy, still lying across Arbert's horse. Cedric carefully lifted him down and laid him on a low wooden seat next to the drinking trough. Wil watched – he didn't know what else to do.

'What happened? Has he said anything since you found him?' asked the girl. She examined the wound on the boy's head and suddenly looked around.

'Where's Farrow? Quick, let me see her. *NOW!*' The girl, who Wil guessed was about fourteen, made everyone jump. Cedric pointed to Farrow, who hadn't moved since she lay down.

The girl knelt down and carefully examined the hound from nose to tail. When she had finished she looked a little happier but didn't say anything. She just went back to the boy.

Cedric did not look happy at all.

'Where's Lady Élanor, Tally? I asked for her! Why hasn't she come?'

'She's with Bryn. Willow's having her pups. One's already died,' answered the girl. 'She sent me to give first aid which, Cedric Tanner, I certainly can do!' She looked at the wound on Seth's head again and started to search though the bag she wore over her shoulder, muttering, 'Damn it! Where's the lavender? I only used it yesterday. Oh, this bag... I... really... must... Ah, at last!'

She held up a tiny glass bottle and dripped a few drops onto Seth's wound.

'This'll clean that wound and stop any infection. Now, take him to the infirmary[10]. I'll look after him until Lady Élanor gets back. Who's this?'

The girl's question took Wil by surprise. He didn't think she had seen him. Cedric reached for his knife.

'We found him when we found Seth. Says he didn't attack Seth. He says that Farrow went to his village to get him. Obviously a lie! A Fellhound would not leave its master! He used magic to control her. Lady Élanor and the Order can have him now.' And with one swipe Cedric cut the rope that tied Wil to Arbert's horse. 'They'll know what to do with him!'

Wil said nothing. He was tired and hungry and he was really hoping he was still dreaming.

The young girl with the silver hair looked straight into Wil's eyes. Her own eyes were the palest blue. She didn't blink. A sudden sharp pain made Wil cry out. He dropped to his knees sure that his head was about to explode. The pain went. He shook his head and gasped. Cedric laughed.

'You think that's bad, boy? Just wait until you meet her sister. Lady Élanor will make you tell the truth – *one way or another!*'

'Take him away!' ordered Tally with another quick glance at Wil. He braced[11] himself for more pain but she looked away quickly. 'I will tell Lady Élanor. She'll see him when she's got time.' She did not look at Wil again. 'Now, take Seth to the hospital and take Farrow to Bryn – *Hurry!* '

CHAPTER FOUR

Saran Jail

Wil sat on the floor in his cell. He was cold, tired and hungry. He was also cross. He picked up tiny stones from the floor and threw them at the wall. Why didn't anyone believe that he had been trying to *help* Seth? He thought about the dead bodies – so much blood.... *errch*!

Just to make sure he really wasn't dreaming, Wil pinched his arm again. It still hurt and his fingers left a bright red mark on his skin. He was definitely awake.

He thought about his mother. It was late; she would be worried. Wil began to wish he'd listened to Garth and waited for the others.

A door at the end of the building creaked open. Silver moonlight lit up the dusty floor and a beautiful young woman with silver hair walked into the jail and shut the door quietly behind her.

Her footsteps made no noise as she walked towards Wil's cell. All he could hear was a dull *thuck, thuck*[12] where she caught each iron bar with her finger as she walked.

There was a sudden movement in the cell nearest to the door. A man ran to the bars. He was spitting and swearing at the woman. She stopped and smiled.

'Ah, Sir Jerad Tinniswood. I see you have not found your manners,' the woman said quietly. She stared straight ahead. 'I will visit tomorrow... we can find them then... and your memory.'

The man pressed his filthy, unshaven face to the bars.

'You will get nothing from me, you evil hellcat! I will die before I tell you anything!'

'So be it,' she whispered and walked on, her long gown brushing softly on the stone floor, her finger flicking across each bar until she reached Wil's cell.

Wil guessed she was Tally's sister, Lady Élanor. He pressed his back right up against the cold cell wall and hoped he would disappear into the darkness.

But he didn't disappear. The woman looked at him through the thick bars. She had the same pale blue eyes as her sister.

'What is your name, boy?'

Her quiet voice made Wil very nervous.

'Wil... Wil Calloway, Ma'am.'

'And how old are you?'

'Seventeen, Ma'am.'

'What did you see, Wil Calloway?'

24

She spoke quietly. Wil tried not to look at her eyes. He answered quickly and hoped that she wouldn't make his head hurt like her sister had done earlier.

'I saw the boy – Seth. Lying on the ground. There were bodies. Then when I woke up I saw Seth's father and the other man. I tried to...'

'*No!*'

Wil jumped. She leant forward.

'What did you see with your mind, Wil Calloway? I know you saw what happened – my sister saw the visions in your head. You saw it all *before* you got there. *Didn't you?*'

Wil didn't know what to say. Should he tell her about his dream? Would he get into even more trouble if he told the truth?

'Yes... No! Um... I, I don't know ...'

Lady Élanor looked into Wil's face. He waited for that terrible pain again. But it didn't come. After a long time she looked away. This time her voice was kind.

'When did you last eat, Wil Calloway?'

'Last night, Ma'am, with my mother – at home.'

'And where is home?'

'Mistlegard, Ma'am.'

'I do not know this place. Where is it?'

'It's on the other side of Mistle Forest, Ma'am. A small farming village.'

'You said you ate with your mother. Where was your father?'

Wil kicked the floor with his foot.

'Five years ago the harvest was very bad. Rexmoore's men came. My parents could not pay their taxes so they took my father. I... eh... I don't know what happened to him after that.'

Lady Élanor stood very still for a long time. Wil didn't look up but he knew she was still looking at him. When she spoke again it was in a whisper.

'I do not believe you tried to kill Seth, Wil Calloway. I think that you tried to help.'

This was wonderful news.

'What? Oh, brilliant! You believe me – really? So, will you ask them to let me out of here?'

But Lady Élanor did not answer and the door was not unlocked.

'Give this boy some food and drink, and a blanket. I will speak to him again in the morning,' she said walking away.

'But... I thought...' Wil started. But she was gone – out through the prison door. The moonlight shone in her hair. Then the door closed and the prison was once more in darkness.

Almost straight away the jailer brought Wil a soft, warm blanket, a huge bowl of hot stew and a large mug of cool ale. Unfortunately the cell door remained locked.

Later, with his stomach full of delicious food, he was nearly asleep when someone crept into his cell and put a pillow under his head. The pillow smelled of summer flowers but he was so tired he couldn't open his eyes. Very soon Wil was fast asleep. And this time he didn't dream at all.

The sound of someone whistling very badly woke Wil. It was light but he could tell it was still very early. The pillow still smelt of flowers and he kept his eyes tightly closed, hoping he would go back to sleep.

The whistling didn't stop.

After a few more minutes Wil sat up. The terrible whistling was coming from Sir Jerad Tinniswood's cell.

'Oh, did I wake you?' said Tinniswood, pretending to be surprised. 'Well, I don't know what you've done, boy, but it was four days before I got more than a mug of water! Either Élanor thinks you're useful,' he paused and with a cruel laugh added. 'Or it was your last meal and they are going to hang you today. So, come on, what did you do?'

'Nothing,' Wil answered. He bashed his pillow with his fist and tried to get comfortable again. 'It's just a big mistake. I'm sure it'll get sorted out today. *I haven't done anything wrong!*'

'So, I'm guessing you have visions,' said Tinniswood. 'Must be important ones if Élanor wants to know? She's mad, of course – and that little sister of hers! I mean, all those herbs and potions can't be good for you. Not that any of them have worked on me yet!'

'Well, I am not mad!' Wil insisted. 'Anyway, why are *you* in here?'

'Now that, my boy, would be telling... and I don't tell!' The man laughed his cruel laugh again. 'Visions, hey? I bet that's useful!'

Wil said nothing. He didn't like or trust this man. Annoyed and unnerved, he laid his head back down on his pillow... and went straight back to sleep.

Wil woke again much later when the jailer's keys clattered[13] against his cell door. This time the man brought a bowl that was full to the brim with steaming porridge. He put it on the floor next to the scented pillow. Right in the middle of the porridge was a blob of cream.

'They want to see you after breakfast. Eat this and try to make yourself look a bit tidier. There's water in that bowl over there.' The tired-looking man pointed to a wide china bowl and a plain blue jug with a large crack down the side that hadn't been there earlier. Wil dipped his fingers into the clear water. Behind him the key rattled in the lock and the man walked away yawning.

The keys jangled again. Wil guessed that Sir Jerad was getting his breakfast, too. But before Wil could blink, porridge and pieces of broken pottery crashed against the bars of Sir Jerad's cell and splattered against the wall.

'Take that muck away! And tell that woman that if she wants me to be helpful she'd better start sending in some decent food!'

The jailer shut the cell door with a crash and locked it. Then he fled. There was a great shout of anger from Tinniswood's cell and then silence.

Wil ate the delicious creamy porridge hoping that Tinniswood might have forgotten about him. But it was no time at all before the man's horrible voice whispered through the gloom, 'Beware of Élanor, boy. Trust me. We could help each other. Lord Rexmoore would be very interested in your unusual talent. He could make you a *very* rich man!'

CHAPTER FIVE

Wil's Trial

Wil was standing in a big hall. It was raining outside and he was damp and cold from the wet walk from the jail house. A balcony opposite him was packed full of people. They were all leaning forward to see the boy who tried to kill Seth Tanner and his precious Fellhound.

Wil started to worry.

Three men and two women were sitting behind a long table at the other end of the room. None of them smiled. The table and the hall looked very old and very shabby[14]. One of the men, the one sitting in the middle, was wearing a dark red cloak with a dark grey fur collar; the other four people were wearing plain black robes. On the wall behind them Wil saw something that made him gasp – the heads of three huge wolves. They looked as if they were charging through the wall towards him, their lips curled back to show long, white teeth. Even in death they looked like they were snarling.

The jailer poked Wil in the back. Wil stepped forwards. At the same time a woman stood up. She was very small and reminded Wil of a sparrow. She spoke to the people at the table.

'Your Worships, Order of the Magewizen of Saran[15], this is Wil Calloway. He is here today charged with the attempted murder of Seth Tanner *and* for stealing forty-three valuable deer.'

People in the gallery shouted. Someone threw a rotten tomato. It landed on the floor with a loud splat! The woman frowned but she didn't say anything.

The man in the red robes ignored the tomato.

'And does he have someone to defend him, Prosecutor[16] Prinze?' The man looked around the hall.

To Wil's total surprise, a cloaked figure at the back of the hall stood up and lowered her hood.

'Lady Élanor,' said the man. He looked very surprised.

'But I...' said Wil, also surprised. But a sudden pain in his head stopped him from saying anything else. It was the same pain he had felt when Tally had looked at him the day before. He looked up. Tally was in the gallery. She was sitting in the corner. Wil looked at Lady Élanor and then back to the gallery. Tally had gone.

The man in the red gown continued.

'As Grand Wizen[17] of the Order of the Magewizen of Saran, I must inform you, Mr Calloway, that you are here today charged with the attempted murder of Seth Tanner and of the theft of forty-three deer. How do you plead?'

He peered over his half-moon spectacles at Wil.

'I… I didn't…' Wil stammered.

'He pleads not guilty, your Worship,' said Lady Élanor, now standing at his side.

'I see,' said the Grand Wizen. 'Well, in that case, Master Calloway, you must stand trial[18] so that we can decide if you are guilty or innocent. Prosecutor, do you need any time to prepare?'

The Prosecutor jumped to her feet.

'No, your Worship, I am ready.'

Wil was confused.

'I, too, am ready, your Worship,' said Lady Élanor, although the calm in her voice did not make Wil feel any better.

The Grand Wizen looked up at the people in the gallery. 'Excellent, in that case we'll start the trial!'

People cheered and clapped. Another tomato flew though the air and hit Wil on the shoulder. It exploded on impact. Bits of tomato dripped down Wil's cheek while the rest plopped onto the floor. A girl giggled. No one got told off.

'Prosecutor Prinze… could you explain the case against Master Calloway?' asked the Grand Wizen.

'Yes, your Worships, I will. Thank you.' The Prosecutor walked to the middle of the room. 'It is very simple, your Worships. Seth Tanner was up at Thesker Fell – on Tel Hireth, your Worships. He had been sent there for two weeks by your Worships as a punishment for something he did earlier. He was there to look after the deer before they went up on to the Fells for the winter.'

The Grand Wizen nodded.

'And how did Mr Calloway become involved?'

Now everyone was listening.

'Yesterday was the last day of Seth Tanner's punishment. He was looking after the deer with his Fellhound, Farrow, when this boy – Wil Calloway,' said the Prosecutor. She pointed towards Wil, 'and four other men, attacked them. Farrow fought bravely. She killed the men, but she and Seth were badly injured in the fight. Calloway used magic to stop the hound from ripping out his throat. Then he tried to murder young Seth. Luckily, Seth's father and uncle arrived and stopped Calloway by knocking him out.'

The Grand Wizen looked shocked.

'And what happened to the forty-two deer, Prosecutor?'

'Forty-three, your Worship,' corrected Miss Prinze. 'Lost. Calloway obviously had more helpers. They took the animals away while the others were fighting.'

'I see,' said the Grand Wizen. 'Well, that is all very clear. Would you like to tell us anything else, Miss Prinze?'

'No, your Worship. I have asked Cedric and Seth's uncle, Arbert, to come in later to tell us what they saw.' She nodded politely and then she sat down in front of a small table at the side of the hall.

'That will be fine. But first I suppose we should hear Mr Calloway's version of events,' said the Grand Wizen. He turned to look at Wil and then spoke very politely to Lady Élanor.

'Lady Élanor, are you going to speak for Mr Calloway?'

Lady Élanor nodded. 'I am, your Worship.'

The Grand Wizen took off his glasses and rubbed his eyes.

'Well, before you start I must ask. Are you happy to do this, Eli? I am worried that this boy might have bewitched you.'

'Your Worship, this boy has not bewitched me,' answered Lady Élanor. 'I wish to defend him because I do not believe he committed this crime.'

'Very well,' said the Grand Wizen. 'If you're sure.'

The Grand Wizen replaced his glasses and turned to the other four members of the Order. They nodded.

'In that case, Miss Prinze, please call your first witness[19].'

With a nod Miss Prinze said loudly, 'First, I would like to call Cedric Tanner, your Worships.'

A door behind Wil opened with a loud creak and a man shuffled in. Tired and pale, he stood just inside the doorway, took his cap off and clutched it in both hands.

'Good morning, Cedric. Come, come in,' said the Grand Wizen kindly. 'How is your son today?'

Wil was amazed. Was this really the same horrible bully who had captured him the previous day?

'Good... good morning, Morten.' The man nodded towards the Grand Wizen. 'Seth's not too good. Lady Élanor says he'll get better, but...' He sniffed loudly. 'Bless him. Lying there. He's white as a ghost and there's nothing I can do to help him!'

Cedric burst into tears and sobbed into his crushed hat.

'I'm sorry. I just feel so helpless,' he wailed.

Prosecutor Prinze rushed forward and gave him a hug.

'I think it might be better to start with Arbert Pernell, Seth's uncle, your Worships,' she said looking at the Order over Cedric's shaking shoulder. 'While Mr Tanner calms down. This is a *very* difficult time for him, especially with his son's attacker standing just over there.'

Lady Élanor was on her feet.

'I must object, your Worships. Seth is not in any danger. As I have already told Mister Tanner, Seth will be absolutely fine. He just needs rest. I must also remind everyone that Master Calloway has not *yet* been found guilty!'

'Yes, quite,' agreed the Grand Wizen quickly. He turned back to the Prosecutor and smiled kindly. 'Annabel – let Cedric sit down. Call Arbert.'

'Yes, your Worship, thank you.' said the Prosecutor. She glared at Lady Élanor. 'Although I think her ladyship's interruption was quite unnecessary!'

'*So were the tears!*' said Lady Élanor under her breath. The Prosecutor's cheeks went pink.

'Your Worships, I now call Arbert Pernell.'

Arbert also crept in. He was already holding his cap tightly in both hands. Cedric took a seat and wiped his nose with his hat. Miss Prince turned to Arbert.

'Mr Pernell,' she said loudly. Arbert jumped when he heard his name. 'Please tell us what happened yesterday on Thesker Fell?'

'Yes, Ma'am, I, er... we... er... we went to see Seth because Cedric was worried about him. His mother – my sister – was worried, too. Hadn't baked a decent loaf since he went – never does when she's worrying. Flat as pancakes–'

The Grand Wizen interrupted, 'Yes, I'm sure, Arbert. But could you just tell us what happened when you got onto the Fells?'

'Sorry, my Lord... I mean, my Worship.' Arbert bowed towards the Grand Wizen and to Miss Prinze. 'Well, we got there late morning. It was really hot and I was glad to get off Daisy because the saddle was really starting to rub my– '

'Mr Pernell!' Miss Prinze interrupted loudly. Her cheeks were now very pink indeed. Wil could see Lady Élanor looking down – she was smiling. The Prosecutor spoke again. 'I think it might be a bit easier, Arbert, if I ask you some questions.'

'Oh, alright, yes,' nodded Arbert.

'Arbert, when you got there, what was Seth doing?'

'Well, nothing, Ma'am. He was lying on the ground... and that boy over there,' he pointed towards Wil. 'That boy was holding a sword over Seth's head. He was going to kill him!'

'Were there any other people there, Arbert?' asked the Prosecutor.

'Well, yes. But they were dead!'

Miss Prinze nodded.

'And did you think that Master Calloway, the person over there, had killed those men?' asked Miss Prinze. She waved her hand towards Wil. Arbert shook his head.

'Oh, no! It was Farrow. She was protecting Seth. She's trained, you know.'

Miss Prinze nodded.

'So, Mr Pernell, if you had not arrived, do you think that Master Calloway would have murdered Seth?'

'Oh yes,' answered Seth, frowning. 'But I hit him over the head and stopped him!' A few people clapped. Arbert grinned and gave a little wave.

The Prosecutor smiled. 'Thank you, Mr Pernell. I do not have any more questions for this person, your Worships.'

The Grand Wizen looked at Lady Élanor.

'My lady, do you have any questions for Mr Pernell?' He asked in a way that suggested he didn't really want her to have any questions. But she did.

'Two questions, your Worship.'

Lady Élanor walked towards Arbert. Wil could see she made him nervous.

'Mr Pernell – Arbert. Are you sure Master Calloway was holding his sword when you saw him with Seth?'

'Um... I'm... um...' the little man began. Speaking slowly, he closed one eye and tried to remember. 'Actually, now I come to think, Ma'am, his sword might have been on the ground by Seth's campfire...'

'So, Arbert, why did you think he was going to kill Seth?' Lady Élanor's voice was quiet and friendly.

'Because Cedric said he was. He told me to stop him – so I did – I hit him with a lump of wood from the fire!' Arbert looked pleased with himself now. He had answered all of Lady Élanor's questions and he hadn't made her cross once!

Lady Élanor returned to her seat.

'I do not have any more questions for Mr Pernell, your Worships.'

Prosecutor Prinze was on her feet before Lady Élanor had time to change her mind.

'In that case, Thank you, Arbert, you can go. Cedric, do you think you're ready now?'

Seth's father moved to stand and then seemed to change his mind.

'Yes, I'm alright now, thank you, Annabel. But can I sit down? My legs are still a bit wobbly.' He started to cry again.

'Would you like some elder wine, Cedric, before we continue?' asked the Grand Wizen.

Cedric blew his nose into his hat and then pushed

it into his pocket.

'No, I'll be fine.'

'Very well, Cedric, if you're sure?... Madam Prinze, please carry on.'

Prosecutor Prinze waited while Cedric sniffed and sighed. The people in the gallery were also silent. Several women dabbed[20] their eyes with handkerchiefs and a man wiped his nose in his sleeve.

Finally, the Prosecutor spoke.

'Cedric, please could you tell us what happened when you arrived on Thesker Fell yesterday morning?'

'Yes, Ma'am. As you know, Arbert and I went up to Tel Hireth to join Seth. But when we got there we couldn't see the deer. Then we saw two men – dead. It was horrible!' He frowned at the memory. 'Then we got worried. We crept up to where Seth was supposed to be watching the animals and we found another dead man. Then we saw Seth lying on the ground. He wasn't moving. And... and that boy there,' he pointed at Wil. 'He was kneeling over my son with his hands around his throat–'

Wil couldn't stop himself. He jumped to his feet.

'I was not. That's wrong!'

'That's enough, Master Calloway!' The Grand Wizen's cheeks wobbled. One of the wizens[21] whispered something to the wizen sitting next to her. He shook his head slowly in reply. Wil was suddenly very angry.

'But I wasn't trying to kill him – I was trying to

help him! I keep trying to tell you! WHY WON'T YOU LISTEN?'

The Grand Wizen banged the table with a small silver hammer.

'Master Calloway, if you do not sit down I will stop this trial and you will go back to the jail until you calm down!'

Wil felt a cool hand on his arm. He thought of his mother.

'It's alright, Wil,' said a voice in his head. Pain prickled behind his eyes. The voice spoke again. *'Everything will be alright but Lady Élanor cannot help unless you sit down. Trust her.'*

Wil looked around him. Lady Élanor's hand was on his arm but her lips weren't moving. Miss Prinze wasn't speaking either. Wil stood very still. The voice whispered again.

'Sit down, Wil. Let my sister help you. Trust her.'

He looked around again. Was he going mad? Then he saw Tally's pale face up in the corner of the gallery where she had been earlier. She gave him a tiny nod. He sat back down. His hands were shaking.

'I must apologise for Master Calloway's behaviour, your Worships. It will not happen again. Cedric, please continue.' Lady Élanor sounded calm but she stayed very close to Wil and kept her hand on his arm.

Cedric continued his story while the Prosecutor walked slowly around the hall.

'I told Arbert to stop him. He was going to murder Seth. After Arbert hit him we tied him up so we could help my boy. When we got back here I called for you, my Lady, but Tally came instead. She looked at the Calloway boy and he collapsed on the floor. Then Tally said to take him away – so we knew we were right!'

The Prosecutor beamed.

'Thank you, Cedric. I have no more questions, your Worships.'

'Lady Élanor?' invited the Grand Wizen. He raised one eyebrow as if he was expecting trouble. The look that Lady Élanor gave Wil told him that any more shouting would be an extremely bad move.

'Thank you, your Worship... Cedric; you said you found the bodies of four men when you found Seth.'

'Yes, Ma'am,' replied Cedric.

'Hmm... and Farrow; she has certainly been trained well and did her job to protect Seth. Yes?'

'Oh, yes, Ma'am. She will die if she has to – that's how they're trained, as you know.' Cedric's voice was full with pride.

'Yes, Cedric, I know. That is why I am wondering why Farrow did not finish her job? You are asking us to believe that this boy was threatening

Seth's life. So why didn't Farrow tear out his throat as she did with the others? That is, after all, what she is trained to do – Yes?'

A few people in the gallery started to murmur. Cedric seemed to be thinking about Lady Élanor's questions but she didn't wait for him to answer.

'The hound sat quietly while you looked after your son, didn't she? She was sitting quietly when you found Wil with Seth, wasn't she?'

Wil could see that Cedric was getting cross but Lady Élanor did not stop asking questions.

'You saw the bodies on Tel Hireth and guessed what had happened, didn't you, Mister Tanner? Wil Calloway was not holding a sword, was he? He was not trying to kill your son, was he? Master Calloway was trying to help. Because that was what Farrow had asked him to do – wasn't it, Mister Tanner?'

'NO!' Cedric shouted, suddenly on his feet. '*HE WAS TRYING TO KILL MY SON, MY ONLY SON! AND I STOPPED HIM!*'

No one in the hall spoke. Cedric was shaking with anger; Wil sat shaking with worry.

Lady Élanor turned away from the gallery and moved towards the long table. Her soft slippers made no noise on the wooden floor as she walked. Even thought it had been raining outside, Wil noticed that Lady Élanor's feet were clean and dry.

'As we all know – and agree, your Worships – Seth and his hound, Farrow, were at Tel Hireth on Thesker Fell while they were looking after the deer. They were attacked by a group of men. Seth was badly injured even though Farrow fought to protect him. So – and this is where we do not agree, your Worships – because she could do nothing for Seth, Farrow left to find help. She found Wil Calloway and led him back to Tel Hireth. Wil Calloway went there to help. He did not know where he was going or what he would find when he got there. He did this to help a stranger. He also stopped a village of frightened people from killing Farrow. Today, your Worships, we should not be wondering if Wil Calloway is guilty or innocent, we should be thanking him for his bravery!'

Lady Élanor's cheeks were very slightly pink when she sat back down. Wil was now very confused. How did she know so much about what had happened? He was trying to remember what he had told her when she had visited him in the jailhouse but the Grand Wizen banged the table with his hammer. Everyone stopped talking.

'Madam Prosecutor, Lady Élanor, do you have any more questions? Or witnesses?'

Both shook their heads.

'Good!' He beamed. 'We will now leave to consider our decision.'

The Order stood up and a voice at the back of the hall said loudly, 'All rise.'[22]

Chairs scraped and boots thudded but no one spoke until all the wizens left the room. As the door shut everyone started talking.

Lady Élanor watched them. She didn't say anything.

'So what happens now?' whispered Wil.

'They will make a decision. Then they will come back in and tell us what they have decided.'

'And how long does that take?'

'Sometimes it can take a very long time... But, today, I think it will not be long.'

'What will happen to me when they come back out?' asked Wil, although he didn't really want to know.

'If they decide that you are guilty you will be hung. If they decide you are innocent you will be free to leave.'

Wil swallowed.

'What, er, what do you think they'll decide?'

He rubbed his ice-cold hands slowly up and down his thighs trying to stop his legs from shaking. Lady Élanor thought for a moment.

'Well... no-one has been hanged in Saran for a long time now – that could go against us.

CHAPTER SIX

The Verdict [23]

A very long time later the door to the Order's room creaked open. A hand appeared and waved. One of the court ushers rushed over, nodded several times, looked at Wil and frowned. The door closed again. In the silent hall everybody waited.

A loud knock from the other side of the same door made everyone jump.

'All rise,' ordered the usher.

There were now a lot more people in the gallery. Everyone stood up. The five wizens came back into the hall. One of them – a thin woman who looked like an eagle – shook her head and sat down. Wil's heart started to beat very fast.

The Grand Wizen's voice was loud in the quiet hall. His kind smile had gone.

'Wil Calloway, please stand.'

Wil jumped up, knocking his chair over. It tumbled backwards; the sound was deafening.

'Master Calloway, you have been accused of attempting to murder Seth Tanner; you have also been accused of stealing forty-three deer. We have listened to the Prosecutor and to the witnesses. We have also listened to Lady Élanor, who has spoken for you,' he said with a polite nod. 'We have discussed what we have heard but we, the Order of the Magewizen of Saran, cannot agree. Some of us think you are guilty; others believe you are innocent.'

The people in the gallery started booing. The usher shouted 'Silence!', but the grumbling rumbled on. The Grand Wizen raised his voice.

'This leaves only one choice.'

The lady who looked like an eagle shook her head again. The Grand Wizen looked over his glasses at Wil.

'You must take part in a test... you will join the Moon Chase in three nights time when the twin moons are full.'

Everybody in the gallery gasped.

'NO!' said Lady Élanor, her face white. 'Morten – he knows nothing of the Chase! This is outrageous!'

But the Grand Wizen continued talking.

'The Moon Chase will be the test. If you survive you will be free to go. Until then you will not leave Saran. Lady Élanor will make sure you get to the Moon Chase when it begins. I now call this trial to a close!'

He banged the little silver hammer on the table and then looked at the other wizens, 'Lunch anyone?'

The Order left the hall immediately but others took a lot longer to go. Everyone wanted to talk about what had just happened. Wil stayed in his seat. He really did not understand what had just happened.

'What's a Moon Chase?' he asked when the hall was empty.

The silver haired young woman looked into his face.

'It is the reason we have Fellhounds, Wil.' Her voice, as usual, was calm. 'The people of Thesk have fed their animals on the Fells for many, many years. But the Fells can be very dangerous, especially Tel Harion. People do not go there very often. Some go and do not come back.'

'What happens to them?' asked Wil, although he really didn't want to know the answer. Lady Élanor's light footsteps could be clearly heard now in the empty room. She walked to the huge table and looked up at the heads above her.

'*The Wraithe Wolves happened to them!*'

'Oh – wolves,' said Wil, sounding relieved. 'There are wolves in Mistle Forest – and wild boar – we hunt them. It's great!'

But Lady Élanor shook her head.

'No, Wil Calloway – not wolves like these! The Wraithe Wolves of Tel Harion are cruel. They have no fear. They do not kill to survive; they kill for fun and they will leave nothing alive once they attack.'

'Oh... *right*,' said Wil. The terrifying heads seemed to be looking right at him. 'Well, remind me never to go up to Tel Harion then!'

'I am sorry, Wil, but that is what the Order has decided that you must do. The Moon Chase is a wolf hunt.'

'*A what... Why?*' demanded Wil.

'Just before Seth was attacked, we lost another herd of deer, near where Cedric found you and Seth. It's close to Tel Harion but the grass there is good. We are sure that these were taken by Wraithe Wolves. They must be stopped before they kill again.'

Wil was suddenly very angry.

'So, these Wraithe Wolves – they must have attacked Seth and Farrow. Maybe they attacked those men as well? I saw the bodies – believe me – a wolf could easily have made that kind of mess!'

'No, Wil. Farrow's wounds were made by a blade, and Tally is sure that the men were killed by Farrow. Fellhounds are trained to bring down their prey and go for the throat; Wraithe Wolves just attack and tear flesh.'

While Wil listened to Lady Élanor he looked up at the three heads with their long dagger-like fangs. Each wolf had *two* sets of teeth, *one behind the other!*

'… and,' Lady Élanor was saying, 'why were they up there in the first place? I believe that those men really were there to steal the deer – most likely for Lord Rexmoore.'

'So… I've got to go on this Moon Chase to find these wolves and kill them?' asked Wil. Then he had a horrible thought. 'Do I have to go on my own?'

'Goodness – No!' said Lady Élanor. 'You will go with the Fellmen. It is their job to hunt the wolves. Your trial is to stay alive.'

'So will I have a Fellhound?'

'No. Fellhounds are very special; they are loyal, working animals that only have one master during their whole lives.'

'But Seth's got one! I could borrow his; he won't be using it, will he?'

'No. Farrow is Seth's hound, Wil. You do not have the experience to use a Fellhound.'

Then Wil had a different worry.

'So what's going to happen to me 'til then?' he asked.

'I think the Order would prefer you to remain in jail but you will stay at my home. You can help Tally with some of her jobs – you will not be bored.'

'And how will you stop me from running away?'

'Wil, if you try to escape the Order will say you are guilty. They will send the Fellmen and their hounds to bring you back – and, Wil Calloway; I can assure you... *they will catch you!*'

CHAPTER SEVEN

Lovage Hall

Lady Élanor's house was much bigger than any house Wil had seen before. It had white walls, a thatched[24] roof and three chimneys. A mouse was foraging[25] in the thatch above the doorway and a jackdaw flew out of a nest on the top of one of the chimneys.

The garden was packed with plants and flowers. It looked like summer. There was colour everywhere, and such wonderful smells – sweet honeysuckle, ripe strawberries, pungent[26] garlic and fresh mint.

'Welcome to Lovage Hall, Wil. Please... come in.'

Lady Élanor pushed the door open. Wil walked into a bright room. Bunches of dried flowers and herbs hung everywhere and right in the middle of a long pine table was a bowl piled high with shiny red and green apples.

At the other end of the room Wil could see a painting above a fireplace. In the painting a handsome man was sitting with a young girl. The man was holding a baby in a pink blanket. They all had silver hair and pale eyes just like Lady Élanor, but the man's eyes were sad.

There was also a huge pine dresser overflowing with tiny glass bottles, more bunches of herbs, candles, books, a basket of eggs... and an enormous black raven.

Wil stared. The magnificent bird let out a loud *Prruk!*

'It's alright, Pricilla,' said Lady Élanor with a smile.

'*Crronk*! Crronk!' said Pricilla. She looked at Wil.

Lady Élanor nodded.

'Yes, this is the boy you saw up on the Fell,' she told the bird. 'He is to take part in the next Moon Chase.'

Pricilla let out another loud 'Crronk!' and flapped her wings.

'Yes, I know. That is why he is here,' Lady Élanor said to the raven. Then, smiling suddenly, she turned to Wil.

'In this house you are innocent[27], Wil Calloway. Please treat it as your home.'

Her smile was kind but Wil couldn't help feeling sad.

'Thanks... but I'm a prisoner really, aren't I? I mean, I can't go home or even let anyone know I'm still alive!' he said. He tried not to cry. He was cross and scared. All he had done was try to help someone who was in trouble. Why had it turned into such a nightmare?

Lady Élanor opened a window and looked at the garden.

'I am sorry for what has happened, Wil. I promise I will do all I can to help you.' She paused. '...If only Cedric had got there before you. Seth is Cedric's only child. There was an older brother but he died before Seth was born.'

'What happened?' asked Wil.

'Fourteen years ago Cedric was travelling back to Saran across the fells with his wife Gwenny, Seth's mother. They had their baby son, Marcus, with them. They were close to Tel Harion but everyone thought it was safe.' Lady Élanor's pale eyes filled with sadness as she told the tale.

'Where was Seth?' interrupted Wil.

'He had not been born.'

'So what happened to Marcus?'

'Cedric's horse fell and cut its leg. Cedric wasn't hurt and as they were close to home Cedric did what he could to stop the blood and continued on foot. But as they went up onto Thesker Fell a full moon appeared from behind a cloud. There, in their path, stood a huge Wraithe Wolf.'

'What happened?' asked Wil.

'Gwenny's horse reared up[28] and Gwenny and

Marcus fell off. The horse ran away and, luckily for the family, the wolf ran after it.'

'So they had time to get away,' suggested Wil.

'Yes. But remember, Wil, Marcus was only a baby. He had fallen a long way when the horse reared. Gwenny realised he wasn't crying. She rushed to him but his neck had been broken in the fall.'

'What happened to him?'

'He was dead, Wil.' Lady Élanor gazed out onto the garden. 'That walk must have been terrible for Cedric and Gwenny – carrying their dead son home when only hours earlier they had been celebrating the second anniversary of his birth.'

'That's really bad,' said Wil. He suddenly felt very sorry for Cedric. Lady Élanor continued.

'About a month later Gwenny discovered that she was going to have another baby. But while she felt joy and hope, Cedric began to worry that something would happen to take this child from him, too. Unfortunately for you, Cedric thought you were trying to do just that.'

Wil opened his mouth to speak but a loud crash and the sound of a girl swearing loudly drowned anything he might have said. Lady Élanor went bright red and ran towards the commotion.

'Tally! *TALASINA! We have company!*'

'*What?*' said a very cross voice. '*Sorry... but the b-blinking chair slipped! Why is the Oil of Cloves on the top shelf anyway? You're lucky I didn't break my neck!'*

Wil followed and found Lady Élanor in the kitchen. On the floor, looking extremely cross, was a young girl covered in white powder. Dried herbs, flowers and pieces of broken pottery were scattered everywhere and a chair lay on its side.

'Oh, my goodness,' cried Lady Élanor. 'What have you broken? I hope it's not the angelica, Talasina? You know how long it takes to collect!'

'No, it's only flour… and just in case you were wondering – I'm fine!'

Wil bit his cheek to stop himself laughing and held out his hand to help the girl to her feet. A flash of pain hit his brain like a lightening bolt. He clutched his head with both hands and cried out. Tally blinked. The pain in Wil's head disappeared.

'I don't need any help!' said the girl crossly. *'And you can stop laughing at me!'*

'I wasn't laughing!' Wil gasped.

'You were – I could feel you laughing at me!'

'That's enough, Talasina!' scolded Lady Élanor. 'Master Calloway was trying to help. Now go and clean yourself up and come back when you are in a better mood!'

Tally scrambled to her feet and left the room, leaving a cloud of flour behind her.

'I must apologise, Wil,' said Lady Élanor.

She tiptoed through the mess. 'Would you like some elder wine... or a herbal tea? Are you hungry? Did you eat the porridge I sent down at breakfast time?'

As she walked the spilt flour seemed to disappear. In a blink[29], three glasses, plates and cutlery were laid on the table.

'Elder wine?' asked Lady Élanor, filling two of the glasses with ruby-red liquid.

Copper pots and pans of every size hung from the ceiling and, just like the living room, herbs tied neatly into bunches, weird-looking plants and coloured bottles filled the walls and shelves.

Wil picked at a thick slice of buttered bread that had just been put on his plate.

'I want to know more about the Moon Chase.'

He was hungry but he couldn't forget the trial.

'Not today, Wil,' said Lady Élanor in a way that really did mean 'Not today'. Then in a much kinder voice she said, 'First I will show you around Lovage Hall – there are places you are free to go and places you must not enter unless you are with Tally or me. We will talk about the Moon Chase properly in the morning.'

Wil liked Lovage Hall. It made him feel safe.

There was a courtyard that you could only get to from the kitchen or the infirmary. The infirmary took up the whole of one side of the building; Lady Élanor and

Tally lived in the rest. The courtyard, like the front garden, was full of wonderful colours and smells. Wil was told not to pick any of the plants because they were all used to make medicines. He was also told that Tally helped in the infirmary where she and Lady Élanor looked after the people from the town when they got ill or hurt.

In the infirmary Lady Élanor let Wil look through the doorway into the ward, but he was not allowed to go in. He could see six beds. There were two children with very bad coughs and a man with a nasty rash all over his face and arms – Lady Élanor told Wil that the man had been stung by a swarm of bees.

In the bed furthest away Wil could see a small bump. The bump didn't move. A woman looked up but then turned back to the bump in the bed. Lady Élanor did not say who was lying there but Wil knew it was Seth.

Back in the main house Lady Élanor showed Wil the room he would be sleeping in during his stay. There were seven bedrooms altogether; one, of course, was Lady Élanor's room and another had a big wooden sign hanging on the door – *TALLY'S ROOM – KEEP OUT!*

The guest room was small and neat.

'Oh, well, at least no-one had to bring up my things,' said Wil feeling angry again. 'Because I haven't got any! Not even my sword!'

Lady Élanor did not say anything. She led the way back down into the room Wil had seen when he first arrived. At the end of the long room was an old ladder. It led up to a balcony packed with more books than Wil had thought existed in the whole world! Lady Élanor suggested that Wil go up for a better look, but the old ladder looked far too rickety[30] so he backed away with a polite nod.

As they were making their way back to the kitchen Wil saw a tiny window across the courtyard that Lady Élanor had not mentioned earlier.

'What's in there?'

'The pharmacy. It is the one place that you are forbidden to enter, Wil.'

'Why?'

'That is where we make our medicines. Some are so powerful that just a sniff could kill you.'

'Can they be used on Wraithe Wolves?' asked Wil hopefully.

Lady Élanor grinned but shook her head.

'We know how these medicines work on people, Wil. But the effect on animals can be very different. Take henbane. An excellent painkiller in tiny amounts, but one of the Fellhounds accidentally ate some once.'

'Did it die?' asked Wil.

'No. It went mad and had to be destroyed. I cannot imagine what could happen if we gave some to a

Wraithe Wolf – they are already vicious killers!'

'Oh,' whispered Wil. 'I'm so glad you told me that!'

The next morning Wil woke in the guest room. He was warm and comfortable and felt a lot better. He had slept extremely well and, lying there, almost believed the previous day had just been a bad dream. Then he remembered that the Moon Chase was one day nearer.

Washed and dressed in some old clothes that had been put out for him, Wil went downstairs into the living room. He could hear voices coming from the kitchen. The front door was open just a crack. Wil stood still and held his breath – he could sneak out now and escape. He thought of his home. His mother would be very worried by now. Suddenly he was desperate to escape. He raised his foot to take a step.

'*THEY WILL FIND YOU! THEY WILL FIND YOU!*' a voice screamed over and over.

Wil put his hands over his ears but the shouting didn't stop – it was *inside* his head!

Then Lady Élanor was shouting. Wil's head was about to burst with pain.

'What are you doing, Talasina? Stop! *Stop this now!* Wil! Wil!'

Wil felt a hand grip his shoulders and then…

The noise stopped.

'What the...? I...' Wil leant forward and put his burning forehead on the cool wall. Lady Élanor rounded on her sister.

'What, by the moons, do you think you are doing, Talasina?'

'He was going to escape! I had to do something! Why do I always get told off when I'm the one trying to help – *oh, this is so unfair!*'

Tally ran back into the kitchen and slammed the door behind her. Wil was still on his knees. He started to shake.

'I'm so sorry, Wil. Are you alright?' Lady Élanor kept her hand on his shoulder. 'Was she right? Were you going to escape?'

'No... I...' He stopped and waited for the terrible pain to return. It didn't. He continued in a whisper. 'I want to go home... I don't want to do the Moon Chase, I haven't got a chance! I just want to go home!'

Tears ran down Wil's face. He leant against the wall and sobbed.

'I just want to go home!'

Lady Élanor stayed close to him.

'I know, Wil. But there is no choice. This is the only way you can be free.'

CHAPTER EIGHT

Lady Élanor Explains

Wil sat at the kitchen table. He was angry and scared. Lady Élanor had gone to look for Tally. A very short, plump woman stirred a steaming pot on the range with a huge wooden spoon. She looked at Wil every now and again and sighed.

Wil had decided that trying to escape was a bad idea, for now at least. If only he could find out who really had attacked Seth, then he wouldn't have to go on the Moon Chase. He would be free and could go home. Just thinking the words *Moon Chase* made him feel sick. He started to imagine what was going to happen. Maybe they would make him stand on the Fell in the dark all alone. Would they wait for the two moons to shine on him to make him easier to find? Maybe they would cut him so that the wolves would be attracted to the smell of his blood? Maybe–

The kitchen door opened and Lady Élanor and Tally walked in. Tally was still sulking.

'The scrambled eggs are ready,' said the woman. 'Are you going to eat with *him*?'

'Yes, of course, Martha,' said Lady Élanor. She smiled. 'Master Calloway is our guest.'

'So you say, but– '

'That's fine, Martha. Tally can finish the eggs. I'm sure they will be delicious. Now, take your husband some breakfast before it gets cold!'

Tally did not look happy about this but moved towards the pan anyway. Martha picked up her shawl and her basket. 'I just don't think that– '

'Thank you for breakfast, Martha. We will see you later. Give Bryn some rosewater; he was looking very tired this morning.'

Lady Élanor held the door open and Martha stomped out. Tally stirred the eggs and served them without saying a word.

As they ate the only sounds were the knife through the bread and the clatter of cutlery – mostly Tally's!

'Wil, we owe you an explanation,' said Lady Élanor eventually. 'And Talasina owes you an apology.'

The sulking girl spoke thought a mouth full of bread and eggs. 'Huh! You only *ever* call me Talasina when I'm in trouble!'

Wil pushed his food around his plate and waited for the next bit of bad news.

Lady Élanor put her hands together and tapped her lips.

'The evening you were brought to Saran Tally looked into your mind. She saw your memory of what had really happened on Tel Hireth.'

'*What?*' said Wil. Then anger welled-up inside him again. *Why hadn't Tally said anything about this at his trial?* But he kept quiet.

To Wil's surprise Lady Élanor answered the question he had not spoken.

'We have a gift, Wil: although Tally sees more detail – sounds, smells. But no-one knows. If they found out about our gift they would accuse us of being witches.'

'So why are you telling me? Is it because I'm going to die anyway, so telling me won't count?'

Wil was standing now. He was angry and confused.

Lady Élanor answered his question although she looked like she was regretting saying anything at all.

'For some reason, Wil, Tally is having a very bad effect on you when she goes into your memories. It's alright when she sends thoughts *to you*, like at the trial. But when she tries to *read* your mind you seem to be fighting her – like you're trying to block her intrusion… Actually, it's quite interesting really.'

'Well, I can assure you – *interesting* is *not* the way I would describe it. It hurts like hell!' Wil was shouting now.

'We can see that, Wil,' replied Lady Élanor. 'And Tally has promised not to go into your mind without warning you – although she probably saved your life this morning – and she certainly helped me to defend[31] you yesterday.'

'*Defend me!.. DEFEND ME!*' yelled Wil. 'How can you say that sending me on a Moon Chase to be torn apart by savage wild animals is a successful defence?'

He sat down hard on his chair and put his head in his hands. Was this nightmare ever going to end?

'Your dream, Wil,' whispered Tally. 'We think you can See, too. We can teach you how to use your gift.'

Wil laughed.

'Great! Well, that'll help to pass the time over the next two days – and I thought I was going to be bored – what with waiting to be killed and all!'

'Wil, that's enough!' said Lady Élanor suddenly. 'Stop feeling sorry for yourself and listen. Believe it or not, we are trying to help you!'

Wil fought the desire[32] to smash a lot of things into very small pieces.

A wasp flew in through the open kitchen window. Wil watched it drift to the table and land in a drip of honey. Stuck fast, it started to buzz with irritation.

BANG! Wil slammed his hand down on the wasp. Tally jumped. Without a word, Wil walked out of the kitchen and out through the front door, which was still open.

Wil didn't hear Lady Élanor approach. He was sitting on the stump of an old tree outside the library, watching a ladybird clamber through an elder bush. He was still very angry. She bent down and let the ladybird climb onto her finger.

'The trial yesterday could have been a lot worse for you, Wil,' she said quietly, watching the ladybird wander over her hand. 'There were so many people there. They wanted you to hang.'

Wil kept his eyes on two jackdaws playing high in the sky above Lady Élanor's head. He did not speak for a long time. Around them insects buzzed and birds sang. On any other day this would be a wonderful place, Wil thought bitterly.

'I don't understand – why didn't everyone just listen to you in the court?' he said out loud.

Lady Élanor spread her fingers. The ladybird flew away towards a thick clump of lavender.

'The people of Saran know that Tally and I have skills they do not understand, Wil, and as long as we use them for the good of the town they make us welcome.'

'So what's this gift I'm supposed to have?' asked Wil.

'Do you remember your dream – the one that told

you that Seth and Farrow had been attacked?'

'Yes.'

'We think you saw it all through Farrow's eyes.'

Wil looked up at her and laughed.

'What? Oh, *riiight*… I can read the minds of animals I've never met before? Never even heard of before?'

'How else do you explain how you saw everything that happened when Seth was unconscious?' As always, Lady Élanor's voice was calm and quiet.

Wil turned the stone over with his foot while he thought about this. His dreams were often strange – in one he had been devouring a sheep in the hills high above Grizzledale and the next day he had heard that a flock of sheep had been attacked in the night, up near the lake.

But he still didn't believe what Lady Élanor was telling him now.

'I don't know – *I just saw it,*' he said irritably. 'Anyway – how is this is going to help me on the Moon Chase?'

'Think about it, Wil. If you can read the minds of the Wraithe Wolves you will know where they are. That will help you in the Chase.'

'*Help?* I thought it was the Fellmen and the hounds' job to kill the wolves – I'm just the bait!'

Lady Élanor laughed out loud.

'*The bait?* I know you think that being sent on the Moon Chase is unfair Wil Calloway. But the people of Saran are not barbarians!³³'

Then she spoke more seriously.

'The hunt is dangerous, Wil. It is a test of your courage and character. You will be there to help the others, not just yourself! If you do that and survive you will earn your freedom.'

'And if I die?'

Turning away from him, Lady Élanor looked at the multicoloured garden.

'If you die fighting you will have proved your innocence, Wil. Die running away and no one in Saran will care.'

Wil pushed his hands through his hair and then looked up at her again.

'And you can help me with this... this mind-reading stuff?'

'Yes.'

'I haven't got a choice then – have I?'

CHAPTER NINE

Fellhounds

Tally came back in a much better mood. The three of them sat at the kitchen table drinking tea and eating a delicious apple cake while Tally talked about Willow and her pups. They were all doing well, although one pup was still very small. Then she started to tell her sister about one of the patients in the infirmary.

'I had to put loads of honey on his porridge before he would even try it!' she said with a frown. 'And he won't drink the hyssop tea – I won't tell you what he said it tasted of!'

'Tell him that it will help take away that headache... tell him that if he will not drink it, I will give it to him another way!' said Lady Élanor in a voice that made Wil silently promise to drink anything that she ever told him to drink. Tally took another bite of her cake and then spoke again.

'His mother told him about the Moon Chase. He wants to go!'

Wil stopped eating. Suddenly his head started to tingle.

'Talasina!' said Lady Élanor, her voice full of warning.

'But he's listening!' said Tally. 'I could feel it!'

'I was not!' Wil lied. 'Anyway, I couldn't.'

Lady Élanor took a sip of her tea.

'I think you should start with an animal that you have read before,' she suggested. 'Come up to the stables. You can try with Willow. She is sleeping a lot at the moment so she shouldn't be too difficult to practise on.'

A short while later Lady Élanor and Wil walked across the courtyard.

'Eli, please will you just check that our patient has actually drunk his hyssop?' Tally called.

Lady Élanor waved to show that she had heard and stepped into the entrance hall of the infirmary. A huge oak door opposite was wide open; beyond it Wil could see a garden and a wood.

'Wait here,' said Lady Élanor, going through another door that she closed behind her.

All alone, Wil looked out at a wood of huge copper-beech trees, each one covered in red and gold leaves. Between the trees a narrow track led up the hill away from the Hall.

Suddenly a loud crash came from the ward.

'I AM NOT DRINKING ANY MORE OF THAT – I

HATE IT! And I *AM* going to the Moon Chase. You can't stop me!'

'You will eat the food that I give you, Seth Tanner, and you will *not* be going anywhere without my say so.' Lady Élanor's voice was cold and hard.

'*I WON'T EAT THIS RUBBISH AND I WILL GO ON THE MOON CHASE!*' screamed the boy. Wil pushed the door. The boy was holding a large white china pot. Lady Élanor was walking backwards with her arms over her head.

Wil ran into the room, straight past Lady Élanor and grabbed the pot from the boy's hand. Luckily it was empty but he kept hold of the boy's arm in case he grabbed anything else.

'Wil! What, by the moons, do you think you are doing?' said Lady Élanor; her face had gone even whiter than usual. The boy stared at Wil.

'*You... you're the one who attacked me,*' he whispered. 'My father told me what happened. *You tried to kill me!*'

'I didn't.' Wil dropped Seth's arm. 'I was trying to save you!'

Wil turned and marched out of the room, out of the infirmary and up the path through the woods. He could hear Lady Élanor's voice behind him but he didn't care, he just kept walking.

Wil didn't stop until he reached the stable block. By the

time Lady Élanor caught up with him she was livid.

'Wil Calloway, didn't I tell you NOT to go into the Infirmary?' she asked, her teeth clenched together as she spoke. 'Did you not understand me?'

'I was just...' Wil started, but Lady Élanor was far too angry to listen.

'You have already been found standing over Seth Tanner's unconscious body once. What do you think his father will say when he hears that you attacked him in his hospital bed?'

'I didn't– ' Wil began. But Lady Élanor wasn't finished.

'I am taking a big risk helping you, young man. In exchange I expect a bit of co-operation. If I ask you *not* to do something I can assure you it is for good reason.' She marched away towards the stables but stopped and turned back. 'Ignore me and you will be lucky to survive *until* the Moon Chase, let alone live through it!'

'...on to six feeds a day now, but– '

Wil walked into the warm, dusty shed and a short, stocky man stopped speaking and looked up. A small, fat puppy lay across one of his arms; Lady Élanor was kneeling next to five more pups sleeping on a bed of straw.

'This is Wil Calloway, Bryn,' she said without looking up.

The puppy in the man's arm nuzzled into his jacket and sucked on one of the buttons. Bryn stroked its tiny ear and looked at Wil.

'Did he do it, Lady E – you know, what they said yesterday?'

'No Bryn, he did not try to kill Seth Tanner – he was trying to help him,' answered Lady Élanor.

'How do you know he's telling the truth?'

'Because Farrow did not kill him,' she said simply.

The man bent down and gently put the sleeping pup back with its brothers and sisters. Then he stepped towards Wil with his hand out-stretched.

'Well, if Farrow thinks you're alright, that's good enough for me!'

He shook Wil's hand.

'Do you want to hold one of the pups, Master Calloway? They were born yesterday; this one's a bit small – but she'll catch up – they always do!'

He scooped up the smallest puppy and carefully gave to Wil. It was warm and soft. 'That's right – hold her under her belly so she feels safe – good. He's a natural, Lady E!'

Lady Élanor nodded but did not smile. Wil could see she was still angry.

'Bryn, the boy needs to spend time with Willow this morning. He can help you with the next feed, too.

I must go down into the town – I will return before lunch-time.'

Bryn led Wil around to another stall. He said that Willow had to be kept away from her pups in case she stood or lay on them.

'If there's time later, I'll take you to see Allana. Her pups are a bit older and a lot bigger than this lot!'

'Who's Allana?' asked Wil.

'Lady E's hound. She used to go on the Moon Chases when she was younger.'

Wil gasped. '*You mean Lady Élanor went on hunts for Wraithe Wolves?*'

'Of course she did! She only stopped when her father died and she had to look after Tally – what with their mother already dead and...' Bryn changed the subject and carried on. 'Tally's got her own hound too, you know!'

'So, does *she* go on the Moon Chases?' Wil asked.

'No. Lady E says she's too young. I don't think she'll ever let her go! She'd be good, too – no fear!'

Bryn opened the gate into Willow's stall. He bent down and patted the hound's shoulder. A chicken in the corner snuggled into the straw and clucked softly.

'Well, girl – you ready for a visitor?' asked Bryn softly. 'Your pups are all asleep so I'll leave you with this young man.' He turned to Wil. 'I'll come and get you both when the pups wake up.' Then he closed the gate and walked quietly out of the barn.

Wil had been in the stall with Willow all morning and now he was cross and uncomfortable. He had tried and tried to read the mind of the sleeping hound but nothing had worked. His knees were sore from kneeling down and his nose was sore from sneezing in the dusty straw.

Lady Élanor and Bryn leant over the door of the stall.

'It's no good, I can't do it!' said Wil. 'I've been sat here for ages but I still don't know what Willow's thinking!'

Lady Élanor opened her mouth to speak but Bryn spoke first.

'The pups'll be due their feed, Lady E. They're making a terrible noise, greedy little things!'

He bent over the gate of the stall and gently poked the sleeping hound. She didn't move. He poked her again. After three more attempts Willow opened her eyes.

Harrumphing and groaning, the sleepy Fellhound got to her feet and stretched. Wil gasped. Willow really was huge. Wil could touch her nose with his without even bending down!

Bryn rubbed her coat with a handful of straw and led her across to the opposite stall. Hearing their mother, the puppies started to yelp – the sound was deafening. Suddenly, Wil wanted to see his mother. He wanted to see her face and hear the sound of her voice.

He could hear Lady Élanor's voice but he couldn't speak.

'Wil, Wil… what's wrong? Why are you crying?'

Wil sank to the floor; he was just about to call out for his mother… when the feeling went. Suddenly he felt safe and warm. Everything was alright.

'What did you do?' he mumbled. The puppies had stopped yelping. They were cuddled up to their mother, all feeding happily.

Lady Élanor smiled.

'I didn't do anything, Wil Calloway,' she replied quietly. 'It was the puppies – you read their minds. They were thinking of their mother so you thought of yours.'

Wil wiped his sweat-soaked forehead.

'How?' he asked.

Lady Élanor watched the pups.

'I don't know, Wil,' she said. 'But I'm sure Tally will be able to answer that one.'

'Well, if you won't let me read his mind, I really don't know how I can help!' insisted Tally. She pushed her mug away, spilling nettle tea across the table.

Wil sat opposite. He stirred his fork around his

bowl of rhubarb crumble but didn't eat any. Tally dipped her finger into the spilt tea.

Wil wanted to know what had happened up at the stables but he really did not want to feel the terrible pain of Tally reading his mind ever again.

'What did you see, Wil?' said Lady Élanor. 'Tell us again.'

'But I keep telling you – I didn't *see* anything. I could just feel stuff. First I felt scared and hungry, then I felt safe and happy.'

Wil frowned.

'I don't think you were reading their minds,' said Tally. She was making swirls in the tea with her finger. 'I think you could sense what the puppies were feeling.'

Wil pushed the bowl away and glared at the two silver-haired girls.

'Great! Well at least I'll know which wolf is going to rip out my throat. I'll be able to sense its strong desire to kill me!'

'Well, that could be useful, Wil,' said Lady Élanor. 'You would know exactly which wolf to fight.'

Wil watched as Tally wrote her name in the spilt tea.

'I want to know what *really* happens on a Moon Chase.' His words surprised him but once he'd said them he was glad – he really did want to know.

Lady Élanor stood up and with a wave of her hand the spilt tea was gone.

'Tally, Nancy Wheeler is coming this afternoon to collect some cough syrup for her new baby. Please go and mix some?'

'I'll go in a minute – I want to hear about the Moon Chase,' objected Tally.

'Tally; go now. She will be here any minute.'

'But, I... '

'I will not ask you again, Talasina.'

Tally banged both her hands on the table and sprang to her feet. Her chair crashed to the floor. She walked out, slamming the door behind her. When she got to the pharmacy, she slammed that door, too.

In the quiet kitchen Wil asked, 'Why don't you want her to hear about the Moon Chase?'

Lady Élanor drummed her slender fingers on the table.

'As you know, Wil, the Moon Chase is a hunt for Wraithe Wolves that have come down off Tel Harion to kill our deer and our sheep. We do not hunt them for fun – they are too dangerous for that.'

'I hope you aren't trying to make me feel better because it isn't working!' said Wil.

'You asked!' replied Lady Élanor.

She then went on to tell him, in detail, about the hunt. She told him about the five chasers who ride on horses, armed with long spears. She told him about the Fellhounds that go with them, and about the bearers –

three more Fellmen armed with crossbows. The bearers wait. The chasers and the hounds go up onto Tel Harion to find the wolf; sometimes the wolf finds them first! The chasers and the Fellhounds chase the wolf towards the bearers. It is their job to kill it as soon as they can.

'So what happens if the bearers get attacked by the wolf?' asked Wil.

'It is the hounds' job to stop that from happening,' answered Lady Élanor. 'A Wraithe Wolf bite is a terrible thing!'

'Why?'

'Because they come from a world of evil, Wil; if you are bitten by a Wraithe Wolf you will suffer terrible agony while you take its form. Then you have no choice but to join the rest of the pack on Tel Harion.'

'What!' gasped Wil. 'You mean if you get bitten by a Wraithe Wolf... *you turn into one? Do you turn back?*'

Lady Élanor poured more nettle tea into their mugs and pushed one towards the stunned boy.

'No. That is why the Moon Chase is so dangerous, Wil. If you get scratched, cut, speared or even shot with a crossbow I can heal you; but if you are bitten there is no potion or spell that will save you from becoming one of the Wraithe Wolves of Tel Harion.'

CHAPTER TEN

Jail Break

Lady Élanor was standing in her living room with a thin, young woman. The woman was holding a crying baby in one arm and clinging on to the elbow of an older child with her other hand. The older child was coughing.

'These two don't give me any peace,' the woman moaned. 'And Cae's no help! Off with that Seth Tanner all the time!'

The woman was Nancy Wheeler. She had come to collect the medicine Tally had made. And from what Wil had heard so far, she had also come to have a good moan. Wil was sitting at the other end of the room by the fire. He was trying to work out what had happened with the puppies but the noise was not helping him to concentrate.

Pricilla, the raven, was perched on the back of his chair.

Wil thought about the Moon Chase. It was the next day. There was no time to practice. Now that he knew he would not be alone, Wil did feel a bit happier.

From what Lady Élanor had said, all he really had to do was not get bitten. Then he would be free to go home at last. His mother would be worried now. His father had been taken by Lord Rexmoore's men five years ago and no-one knew if he was alive, or dead. Now Wil's mother probably thought Wil had been taken, too.

Suddenly Wil heard a voice.

'She will see you again. You must be brave and strong. But do not think you are going just to watch, Wil Calloway. Do not underestimate the power of the Wraithe Wolves.'

Wil looked around. Nancy Wheeler was still moaning to Lady Élanor. The little boy was still coughing.

Pricilla flew down off the chair and landed on a low stool by Wil's feet. The voice came again.

'Trust your senses, Wil Calloway. They will save your life.'

The raven tapped Wil's boot twice with her huge bill, glared at him with her beady black eyes and took off towards an open window. The sound of fluttering feathers made both women look.

'OOH! Is that the boy from the trial?' shrieked Nancy.

She pointed down the room with a bony finger. Wil sat back into the chair and tried his best to become invisible. 'He should be in the jail after what he did to that poor boy! Nearly dead, I heard. I pity his mother. Already lost one son and–'

Lady Élanor raised her voice above Nancy's shrieking.

'Well, I believe him to be innocent, Nancy. And as you already know, Seth is not going to die. In fact he will be going home very soon. We do not know who attacked Seth, AND, as you are married to the jailer I am sure you know that I am trying my best to find out who was!'

Nancy looked back at Lady Élanor and opened her mouth. But Lady Élanor picked up a large blue medicine bottle that Tally delivered earlier and opened the front door.

'Give this syrup to your children three times a day for a week. If they are still coughing then, come back and see me.' She put the bottle into Nancy's hand and held the front door open. As soon as the nosey woman stepped off the doorstep Lady Élanor shut the door behind her.

Wil heard Nancy mutter, 'Well, really!', as she dragged her sickly children away down the garden path.

As the sound of crying and coughing faded away Tally

rushed in through the kitchen door; her cheeks were bright red and she was completely out of breath.

'Eli, Eli – he's gone! He's escaped!'

'What? Who's gone? Wil is still here, look.' She pointed towards the fireplace.

'No!' shouted Tally. 'Sir Jerad Tinniswood! He's escaped from the jail, Eli... and he tried to take Tanith!'

Lady Élanor went white. She headed for the courtyard, talking as she walked.

'Where is Tanith now? How did this happen? Is Tanith alright?'

Tally ran after her. Wil followed them both.

'Horace Wheeler fell asleep... Tinniswood picked the lock... he tied Horace up!' Tally was saying as she chased after her sister. By now she was quite out of breath. But Lady Élanor did not slow down. 'He knocked Bryn out... Willow stopped him... taking Tanith... Eli... Tanith is alright... I've given Bryn... some centaury... he's got a... nasty bang on... his head.'

Lady Élanor ran into the stable block but did not stop until she got to the very end stable. A golden horse appeared over the stall door and whinnied softly.

'I told you Tanith was okay, Eli... '

Tally held her side and gasped for breath. But Lady Élanor wasn't out of breath at all. She gently stroked Tanith's neck and spoke very quietly to the horse. She spoke in a strange language that Wil could not understand. The horse blew short breaths through his soft nostrils.

After a few moments, Lady Élanor seemed happy that the animal really was alright and turned to her sister.

'Where's Bryn?'

'We took him to the infirmary. Martha's with him. She found him lying in the yard. He'd been knocked out. Didn't you hear Willow barking? I heard her from the pharmacy!'

'No, Nancy Wheeler and her children were making far too much noise!' said Lady Élanor. She stroked Tanith's nose. 'How did you know about Tinniswood?'

'The new wizen, Fermina Fairfax. She was coming to the Hall to tell you but she heard Willow and came straight up here instead.'

'Where is she now?' asked Lady Élanor looking around as if she expected Fermina to appear.

'With Martha and Bryn. Martha's very upset.'

'Hmm,' Lady Élanor frowned. 'Finding unconscious people being protected by Fellhounds is becoming a bit of a habit around here. Well, thank goodness you were with me, Wil. At least the Order won't be able to blame you this time!'

Back in the kitchen of Lovage Hall Martha and Fermina

Fairfax were sitting at the kitchen table. Both women looked pale and shocked. Lady Élanor returned from checking on Bryn.

'I gave them some elder wine,' Tally whispered to her sister. 'They looked like they needed something a bit stronger than tea.'

A loud bang on the front door made Fermina jump; she knocked Martha's glass across the table. But before Wil could blink, Lady Élanor caught the glass without spilling a single drop.

Tally went to the door to find Grand Wizen Morten Mortens, Oswald Beck, Agatha Peasgood and a cross-looking man Wil found out later was named Godwyn Savidge. Tally showed them into the living room where Fermina Fairfax was already sitting with another glass of elder wine in her hand.

'Well, I don't think it's a good idea to have this young Calloway lad so close to the boy he attacked!' said Agatha Peasgood, her expression full of disapproval.

'This has not yet been proved, Agatha,' said Lady Élanor. 'And, anyway, Seth will be going home first thing in the morning.'

'Well, as long as he will *not* be joining the Moon Chase, that is good news,' said Godwyn Savidge. He looked no happier than when he had first arrived. 'Giles has been training hard for this hunt and I do not want him in more danger than is necessary. I've *never* been happy about that Tanner boy joining the Chase – too weak, if you ask me! Have you seen–'

'With all due respect, Godwyn,' interrupted Lady Élanor with a polite smile. 'But I thought we were supposed to be discussing Sir Jerad Tinniswood's escape from Saran Jail?'

'I agree,' said Fermina Fairfax. She peered into her tea cup in a way that suggested that she would rather have another glass of Lady Élanor's elder wine.

The Grand Wizen poured himself more tea. 'I think the most important question right now is *Where* is he? The Moon Chase is tomorrow night and five of our precious Fellhounds will be going. If Saran is attacked while they are away… ' He shook his head.

Fermina Fairfax interrupted.

'Lady Élanor, I understand you could not get any information from Tinniswood?' She leant forward and took a piece of cake, inspected both sides carefully and then took a tiny bite from one corner.

'I– ', Lady Élanor started. But Morten Mortens spoke.

'Lady Élanor spent only a very short time with Sir Jerad because other events have taken her attention.' He glanced at Wil.

'Hmm!' sniffed Fermina. 'Well, as we don't know where Sir Jerad is, *or* what he knows, I really can't see how we are going to be able to defend ourselves!' She paused, and then said, 'And what if he has discovered the whereabouts of Lord Lakeston's legacy?[34]'

'No, no. I can assure you it is well hidden and heavily protected,' said Morten. 'Only three people know where it is and I do not for one minute think that Sir Jerad is one of them.'

'But what if something happened to one of the *mystery* three? Would it not be wise to share this secret with us, your *trusted* Order?' suggested Fermina helpfully.

'I would not like to put the Order in any danger by asking them to keep such a secret. Don't worry, Fermina, the legacy is very well protected.' Morten smiled politely again and helped himself to his third piece of cake. Wil could see that the subject of the legacy was now closed to further discussion.

There followed a long debate[35] about whether the Moon Chase should be delayed until Sir Jerad was re-captured or until they found out where he was; but eventually they agreed that it should go ahead. If the stolen deer were still alive on Tel Harion it was only a matter of time before the Wraithe Wolves killed them all.

Wil wasn't sure how he felt about this. He really did not want to go on the hunt but he really did want it to be over so that he could go home.

Chapter Eleven

Morning Visitors

Wil sat in front of yet another uneaten meal.

'Are you going to eat that?' asked Tally.

'Er... No – thanks – I'm not hungry – think I had too much of Martha's honey cake earlier.' He pushed the plate away and sat with his arms folded across the table, staring at nothing.

'Are you afraid? You know – about tomorrow night?' Tally looked at her hands as she spoke.

Wil didn't answer. He really didn't want to talk about it. Tally got up.

'D'you want some elder wine?'

She dragged her chair across the floor, pulled her skirt over her knees and hopped-up to get two goblets from the highest of the kitchen shelves. Then, after filling them both with wine, she put one in front of Wil and sat back down opposite him.

'Do you think Lady Élanor'll let you go on a Moon Chase when you're older?' Wil asked. 'I mean, you've got your own Fellhound. Bryn told me.' He sipped the sweet drink; it made him feel warm as he swallowed.

'She'll *never* let me hunt,' answered Tally. 'Pickles is more of a pet really.'

Wil choked on his wine.

'*Pickles!*'

Tally's cheeks went pink.

'I was very young when Eli gave him to me. Anyway, he's used to it now!'

'Well, maybe Lady Élanor doesn't want you to hunt with him in case people laugh!'

Tally slammed her glass down on the table. Elder wine splashed over her hand.

'Look, I'm sorry,' Wil said quickly. 'I'm sure Pickles is lovely. But you do have to admit that it's a bit of a strange name for a Fellhound.'

Tally wiped her hand in her skirt.

'So what's this legacy?' Wil asked in an attempt to change the subject. He took another sip of his drink. Tally was still sulking but at least she hadn't left the room! Wil asked another question.

'Who was Lord Lakeston?'

Tally looked suddenly sad.

'Lord Lakeston ruled Thesk before Rexmoore. He was our father. He's dead.'

'Oh, I'm sorry. How – when – did he...?' asked Wil. He regretted asking the question.

'My mother died giving birth to me. My father missed her terribly. After she died he just gave up.

He died when I was five. But by then Lord Rexmoore and his wife Imelda, my mother's sister, had already taken all of my father's land and the power that went with it.'

'How did you end up living here, in Lovage Hall?' asked Wil.

'Eli looked after me after my mother died; Father bought Lovage Hall to keep us out of Rexmoore and Imelda's way. He helped Eli to set up the infirmary for the town. Imelda hates Eli because of her power – she doesn't know about mine.'

'So the legacy was Lovage Hall?'

'Sort of – I don't really know. Our father made sure that we would always have enough gold to keep the Infirmary going and to live here... so that we never had to ask Imelda for anything. She's selfish and greedy. Rexmoore's ever increasing taxes are used to pay for her *very* expensive lifestyle. She doesn't care about the people of Thesk at all.'

'So the legacy's the gold? Rexmoore wants it and he sent Tinniswood to find it.'

Tally took a gulp of wine and nodded.

'I think so. But only three people know where the gold is... and, before you ask – No, I am not one of them.'

It was still very early in the morning when Wil finally gave up trying to go to sleep. He got up. A baggy tunic and a pair of trousers had been left for him during the night while he had been sleeping. He put them on and went downstairs.

Nobody else was up and Lovage Hall was silent. He wandered into the kitchen. Outside it was windy and Lady Élanor's plants bowed their heads under the weight of heavy rain. A dark figure came out of the infirmary. At first Wil thought it was Lady Élanor, but the figure stayed very close to the wall and moved slowly towards the pharmacy. Whoever it was, they were wearing a big, dark green cloak. But as they got closer, Wil could see that it wasn't Lady Élanor, or Tally. He held his breath and watched.

After a few seconds the bolt on the pharmacy door scraped open. Without thinking Wil grabbed the nearest frying pan and banged it down hard on the range. *CLANNGGG!*[36]

The mysterious visitor was pelting back across the courtyard just as Lady Élanor and Tally rushed in from the living room. By the look of Tally's very messy hair Wil guessed she had been sound asleep.

'By the moons, Wil, what are you doing?' demanded Lady Élanor.

Wil spoke quickly. 'Someone in the garden. In the pharmacy. Not Martha. I didn't know what to do!'

'Was it Sir Jerad, Wil?' demanded Lady Élanor. 'Did he get into the pharmacy?'

'No. I don't know.' Wil was standing on his tip-toes trying to get a better look across the wet courtyard. Lady Élanor was already half-way out through the kitchen door when she stopped.

'Tally, take Wil up to the stables. Check everything is alright. I'll check on Seth and Bryn.'

Tally raced upstairs to get dressed. When she re-appeared she was carrying a grey woollen bundle that she handed to Wil.

'You can use this cloak. It might be a bit big but it'll be useful on the Moon Chase. Get your boots – *come on!*'

She sprinted across the courtyard to the infirmary. Wil followed but the cloak was quite difficult to put on because it was very big and very heavy. By the time he got across the courtyard Tally was almost out through the big oak doors. But Wil stopped. A long, dark green cloak was hanging on one of the iron hooks in the hallway. It was dripping wet.

'That cloak, look. That's what the intruder was wearing!'

Tally looked even more worried and set off again.

'Come on! I really think we need to check the stables!'

Willow didn't even lift her head when Wil peered[37] into her stall. Tally had ordered Wil to go straight to Willow and her pups while she went to check that Tanith was alright. They needn't have worried. Willow was snoring and the puppies were dozing in the warm straw of their own bed.

'Oh, thank goodness. Tanith's fine, too,' breathed Tally. 'Come on, we'd better check on the others.'

But as she spoke Bryn appeared in the doorway.

'Thought I'd find you here! Allana and Pickles are fine, and Allana's pups. Been to check them myself, just now.'

'Bryn!' said Tally in surprise. Then she frowned. 'Did my sister say you were well enough to come up?'

'I'll be fine, missy. Lady E told me about the mystery visitor though.' There was a bruise the size of an apple on the man's temple. He frowned. 'It was strange but I put my cloak on to come up here, just now and look, its wet.' He held out the edge of the cloak for them to see.

'Well, it would be too big for me, Bryn, and as you can see I found old Monty Barrowman's cloak for Wil,' said Tally.

Bryn opened his mouth to say something but a young man's voice called his name before he could speak.

'BRYN! *BRYN!* Where are you man?' The voice sounded cross and Bryn did not look happy to hear it. He slowly turned his head.

'Giles Savidge, what are you doing up here?'

Bryn didn't move from the stable doorway so Giles couldn't see who was inside.

'I need some more of those silver-tipped crossbow bolts for the Moon Chase tonight,' said the boy. His voice reminded Wil of Godwyn Savidge; it was rude and arrogant. Wil could just picture Giles walking around the yard like a cockerel showing off in front of the hens.

'I've been training hard for this and *I know* I'm going to need more,' continued Giles. 'Especially now we'll have that villain with us. You know? The one who tried to kill Seth Tanner. So, old man, have you got any bolts, or not?'

'I've got three but you'll have to pay me now. You still owe me for the last lot,' Bryn growled.

'Look, just give me the bolts. I'll send the money up later; although you could ask Lady Élanor to pay you out of her precious legacy!' Giles stopped talking, but then added, 'Don't worry, old man. I'll bring you the body of my first Wraithe Wolf. You can take the bolts back for yourself!'

He went off laughing.

'What!' Tally gasped. 'I can't believe he just said that!'

'Don't worry, young Tally. He was joking,' said Bryn. They watched Giles stride[38] away through the beech trees.

'Yes, but Bryn, even to make a joke… bringing the body of a Wraithe Wolf into Saran – we'd have all of the Tel Harion wolves down here before the sun came up!'

'I'm sure he was joking, Tally,' said Lady Élanor after her sister had told her what Giles had said to Bryn. Tally was still very upset.

Wil was once again standing in the hallway of the infirmary. The door to the ward was open a crack. Wil looked in. He could see Tally and her sister. Seth had been sent home and all of the beds were now empty; each one covered in clean white linen ready for the next patients to arrive.

'He was so rude, Eli.'

Lady Élanor put her arm around her sister and stroked her hair.

'I will speak to Morten before the Moon Chase tonight. Giles must be reminded exactly what a Bearer's job is. Pricilla will fly with them, too. Saran will be safe, don't worry.'

Tally stepped back and looked up into her sister's face.

'And Wil? Will he be safe, too?'

Lady Élanor gave her sister a hug and looked straight at Wil.

'As long as he keeps his mind open, as well as his eyes, he will be fine.'

The loud bang at the front door was answered by Martha this time. Wil listened. He heard a man's voice and then he heard Martha.

'But he's not packed yet! No, wait. Don't go in there!'

Two men armed with broadswords marched into the kitchen; one was holding Martha's arm as she tried to stand in their way.

'M'lady, they've come for Wil!'

Lady Élanor and Tally were on their feet in a blink; Tally opened her mouth but Lady Élanor spoke first.

'Gentlemen, you are earlier than expected.'

'We are under orders from the Grand Wizen, Ma'am. Calloway is to come now to stop him trying to contact Sir Jerad Tinniswood before the Chase, Ma'am.'

'*What!*' said Lady Élanor, Tally and Wil, all at the same time.

Lady Élanor went so white that, with her silver hair. She looked like a ghost.

'This is a mistake, Wil. Stay here with Tally. I will go and speak to the Order.'

'No!' said Tally. 'I think *I* should go and speak with them!'

She stepped towards one of the guards. Wil grabbed her arm.

'Tally, please. Look, these men are only doing their job. I'll go with them. I haven't packed and I don't know what I'm supposed to have. Could you... er... could you bring some stuff down for me later... *please, Tally?*'

Tally looked like she was about to argue, but didn't. She shook his hand away and looked at the floor.

'Wil's right, Tally,' said Lady Élanor, wrapping her long silver cloak around her shoulders. 'We'll go now and you can bring Wil's pack down later.'

The guards gave her a grateful bow.

Lady Élanor pulled her hood over her head and whispered something to Martha. Then she and Wil followed the guards out of Lovage Hall. It was raining again.

CHAPTER TWELVE

An Early Start

They were back in the Great Hall. The heads of the three Wraithe Wolves looked down; Wil was sure they were laughing. Fermina Fairfax was sitting at one end of the long oak table looking very pleased about something.

All four wizens; Fermina Fairfax, Godwyn Savidge, Oswald Beck and Agatha Peasgood were there with Grand Wizen, Morten Mortens. Lady Élanor stood in front of them. She did not look pleased; she looked very, very angry.

'This action is deeply insulting, Morten. For the past fifteen years my sister and I have done our best to help the people of Saran. Many of your children are alive today thanks to *our* medicines.'

'Many children in *many* other towns survive without your help, my Lady!' said Godwyn Savidge.

'Do I need to remind you, Godwyn, that your son Giles would *not* have been one of those children?' said Lady Élanor.

'If I could just step in,' interrupted the Grand Wizen. 'I am sorry if you have been offended, Lady

Élanor. But Wil is here now so there seems little point in sending him back up to the Hall. The other's are already here anyway.'

Wil knew the Grand Wizen was right but he could tell that Lady Élanor was still not at all happy, especially after what Godwyn Savidge had said. He was just relieved that Tally had not been there, too!

Outside it had stopped raining. To Wil's surprise they didn't go into the jail; instead they marched around the corner into a huge yard. Wil gasped.

The yard was full of brightly coloured tents and flags fluttering in the breeze. People were laughing and joking; some were drinking from huge jugs of beer.

Wil's mouth was suddenly very dry.

'Don't worry, Wil; this is not all for you. People have travelled here from all over Thesk for this. Their animals are also in danger from the Wraithe Wolves. The Moon Chase is to start from here because our deer were the first to be attacked.'

A loud bark echoed around the yard. Next to the jailhouse Wil could see six fully-grown, *absolutely massive* Fellhounds – each one wearing a cast iron collar. Close by, a group of young men and women were talking and laughing. They were all dressed in thick leather and chainmail suits. One was taller than the others; he had a broadsword that glinted in the sunshine. Others had crossbows; some held long spears. Godwyn, Fermina and Oswald went straight over to join the group and were welcomed with lots of back-patting[39] and hearty-hugging[40].

'Are they the Fellmen?' whispered Wil. They looked like athletes. He suddenly felt very small.

Lady Élanor nodded.

'Don't forget, Wil. This is not a game. They will only survive if they are fast and strong.'

'There you are! *I've been waiting ages!*' said a waspish[41] voice. Tally was trying to get through the crowd and she still looked very cross. She was struggling to carry a long bag which she threw down next to Wil's feet. It landed with a thud.

'Did you find out why they came for Wil so soon?' Tally asked. But before her sister could answer, a loud shout from the Fellmen made them all look around.

A young man was getting down off a beautiful black horse. He turned to the crowd. Wil gasped. The young man had a terrible scar across his left eye, and part of his nose and his left ear were missing!

Tally scowled.

'I see Giles is still popular – *despite everything*! Look at him on his father's horse, huh! He's pretending to be a chaser!'

'Is that the boy who came to see Bryn this morning – Giles Savidge?' whispered Wil. 'What happened to his face?'

'That depends on who you believe, Wil!' said Tally. 'Giles thinks he's too good to be a Bearer. A few years ago he left the other bearers and followed the chasers up onto Tel Harion during a Moon Chase. Somehow Giles got trapped and attacked. He was very lucky. Eli saved him. If she hadn't helped him he would now be up on Tel Harion with the other Wraithe Wolves!'

Wil glanced at Lady Élanor.

'Is that what you meant earlier when you said that Giles wouldn't have been one of the lucky ones?'

'Yes, Wil.' She watched the Fellmen. 'By the time they got him to Lovage Hall his wounds had become infected. I did my best but the damage had already been done.'

'I don't understand,' said Wil. 'Why are they treating him like a hero? He put everyone in danger. You saved him but his father was rude to you!'

Lady Élanor watched Giles showing off.

'Giles told everyone that the other bearers had made a mistake. He said that they had driven the wolf towards him and that he'd been injured trying to kill the wolf on his own. It is true that the wolf had been killed but it was impossible to say who had killed it because all of the bearers shot at it when they found it with Giles.'

'But why didn't the others just tell the truth?'

'They tried, Wil. And I knew the truth because I saw it in Giles's mind while he lay near to death in the

Infirmary; the truth was that he had disturbed a mountain lion when he climbed through the rocks. She gave him those scars. The wolf found him after!'

'So why didn't you just tell everyone what you saw?'

Lady Élanor turned to Wil at last.

'You tried to tell the truth and look where it got you!' she replied. 'Unfortunately the two bearers, Cae Wheeler and Ellyn Parry, do not have rich fathers who are also members of the Order. Giles's father, Godwyn Savidge is both. He buys the Fellmen silver-tipped bolts, new crossbows, spears, saddles and the leather and mail suits they wear today. Oh, yes, he made sure everyone believed Giles' story!'

'But you said that if you were bitten by a Wraithe Wolf you turned into one. If everyone knows that and Giles *didn't* turn into a wolf, well that would have proved he was lying?'

'The wolf was standing over Giles when they found him; in the darkness no-one could really see what was happening but I found no tooth marks. Maybe it licked Giles's wound, I don't know. But I know that Giles didn't turn into a wolf that night because he wasn't actually bitten by one!' said Lady Élanor quietly so that no-one else could hear. 'People chose to believe Giles because it gave them hope that there is actually a cure for a Wraithe Wolf bite. Giles just kept telling his story until everyone believed him. He became a hero. They didn't want to believe anything else.'

'So what happened to Cae and Ellyn?'

'Cae still hunts but he is bullied by Giles and Leon Beck, over there.' She nodded towards a shorter young man with blond curly hair. 'Ellyn and her family moved away. She has not been on a hunt since that night.'

'So will Cae be on the Moon Chase tonight?'

'No. Tonight the Bearers will be Giles, Leon Beck and Fermina Fairfax's daughter, Gisella.'

Wil's heart sank[42].

'Oh, great! So, all of the people with the crossbows are all related to the people who think I tried to kill Seth Tanner!'

'I'm sorry, Wil. I have only just found out. But Leon and Gisella are excellent Bearers. The five Chasers will be Mortimer Merridown, Emmet MacPhee, Curtis Waller, Becky Lum and Olivia Drews. They are all experienced Fellmen – and no, none of them are related to Seth Tanner. Mortimer will be team leader – he is very fair. Do exactly as you are told and you will come back a free man.'

'Lady Élanor, could you bring your *guest* over now?'

Morten Mortens called out. Everyone stopped talking. Giles said something to his companions; they

103

laughed. Then Giles's father said something else. They laughed again.

Wil pretended not to notice. He grabbed the strap of the bag that Tally had brought down from Lovage Hall and swung it over his shoulder. Its weight took him by surprise and he nearly fell over sideways. One of the chasers giggled.

'Blimey, Tally. What's in here?' Wil hissed.

Tally looked hurt.

'Some food – chicken pie, bread and honey cake from Martha; a flask of water and the cloak that I gave you this morning... '

She bit her lip and went on.

'There's also a first aid bag... Eli and I... we made it for you last night after you'd gone to bed. Its pink silk, sorry, that was all I could find. Oh, and Bryn said "Good Luck".'

'Er, Thanks,' said Wil. 'But first aid? I don't know anything about herbs or potions, so, er... '

'Don't worry about that Wil,' said Lady Élanor. 'Trust the– '

A loud cheer drowned out whatever she said next. The five Chasers had mounted[43] their horses and were waving to the crowd.

Wil noticed that there weren't any more horses.

'Do the Bearers walk?' he asked.

'No, they ride with the Chasers,' answered Tally.

She turned to him, her face suddenly worried. 'You can ride, can't you, Wil?'

'Er – No – and I hate heights!'

'*What!*'

'It's never been a problem before!'

'Well, it could be now!' said Tally. 'We were worrying about how you'll survive the Moon Chase, not how you're going to get there!'

'Master Calloway. You'll ride with Olivia,' announced Morten Mortens. Olivia did not look pleased.

After two failed attempts Wil managed to get on, although he did nearly end up facing the wrong way!

'Unless you put your arms around my waist, you will be on the floor again very shortly!' said Olivia impatiently.

'Oh, right,' said Wil. He carefully put his hands around the girl's waist. Her hair smelled of honey and lavender. It tickled his nose but he was much too nervous to move back.

Godwyn Savidge stepped in front of the Grand Wizen.

'Ladies and Gentlemen, silence please! The time has finally come. Our champions must go out onto Thesker Fell to protect the people of Saran and its neighbours. They face great danger but they go with bravery and courage in their hearts.

'Today they take with them Wil Calloway.'

People booed and hissed at Wil's name. Godwyn waited. The crown fell silent again.

'If he dies on Tel Harion his guilt will be proved,' Godwyn continued, looking directly at Lady Élanor. 'If he comes back *unharmed*, the Order will declare him innocent and he will be free to leave.'

The crowd murmured.

'BUT,' Godwyn held up his hand. 'If he returns injured in any way, this will also prove his guilt and he will hang by the neck until dead!'

The crowd cheered. Lady Élanor grabbed the Grand Wizen's arm.

'What! Morten, when did the Order decide this?'

The Grand Wizen looked nervous. Wil felt sick.

'It was the others, my Lady – I really am truly sorry.'

At that moment a huge, black cloud covered the sun. The crowd continued to cheer. The champions smiled and waved. Lady Élanor fixed Wil with her pale blue eyes.

'Remember, Wil Calloway, use your skill and you will go free – I promise you!'

Moon Chase

CHAPTER THIRTEEN

The Friendless Journey

In some ways Wil was pleased to be leaving Saran. He dreaded the Moon Chase but seeing Mistlegard Forest in the distance made him feel just a bit closer to home.

'The moons are rising!' called Mortimer Merridown. He was the only one riding alone. 'Should give us some decent light for the chase!'

'How long will it take us to get there, Mortimer?' asked a tall, thin girl who rode holding her reins in one gloved hand.

'Probably a couple of hours, Becky,' answered Mortimer.

The girl riding with Becky Lum, Will guessed, was Gisella Fairfax. He noticed that she was pretty but, like her mother, she didn't seem to smile much.

'Not if we gallop!' shouted Giles. He was sitting behind a dark young man who grinned at Giles's suggestion.

'No, we don't want to tire the horses before we get there, Giles.' Mortimer glanced at Wil who was clinging on to Olivia. 'And I don't think our *guest* has done much riding!'

'By the way he's squeezing the breath out of me, I'd say he's *never* been on a horse before in his life!' wheezed Olivia.

A handsome grey horse trotted alongside them. It was being ridden by another two young men. Wil guessed they were both older than him.

'So, did you get any more bolts, Savidge?' called the one at the back.

'Yep!' Giles grinned. 'Old Draxton wasn't too happy. Reckons I owe him eighteen shillings, Leon! I told him my father would pay – shame I forgot to tell my father!'

Leon Beck and Giles both laughed. Wil was beginning to understand why no one at Lovage Hall liked this young man.

After a very long time, Mortimer reined-in[44] his horse. Everyone else stopped, too. It was dark now but Wil could see huge rocks and trees in the moonlight.

Mortimer slid down from his horse.

'We'll camp here. MacPhee, can you make a fire?'

Emmet MacPhee nodded. Giles started to show off again.

'You know, we really should ask my father to employ someone to do all this boring stuff before we get here! I'm starving. Anyone got any food?'

'Honestly, Giles. How many times have we told you – you really should bring food with you!' said Olivia. But she was smiling as she dismounted and handed Giles a small bag. He grabbed it, pulled out a loaf of bread and bit right into the middle of it.

Olivia looked hurt.

'That was for both of us, Giles!'

But Giles just took another enormous bite and opened his mouth to show her the half-chewed bread.

Wil watched. He did not want to get off the horse; he was very stiff and it was a long way down! Seriously worried that his legs might not work ever again, he carefully slid from the saddle. Riding, he decided, was definitely not for him!

'So, where's your food, Calloway?' But Giles didn't wait for an answer. With his mouth still full of bread, he grabbed Wil's pack.

'Oh, I... I don't know,' said Wil. 'They packed it for me.'

'Well, let's see... ooh, a nice warm cloak.' Giles held up old Mister Barrowman's cloak then dropped it into the dirt. 'Oh, and a pink wash bag... silk, *niiice!*'

With a horrid laugh, he threw the little bag over his shoulder. It landed right in the middle of a thorn bush. Wil was starting to get angry.

'Oh, at last! Pie, yum! My favourite!' said Giles.

He let go of Wil's pack, trod on it, and walked away taking huge mouthfuls of the pie.

Wil stepped forward and grabbed up the cloak and the pack, which now had a big muddy foot print on it. He reached in and found a piece of Martha's honey cake and a loaf of bread. The cake was squashed flat. Wil really was angry now. He turned and hurled the squashed cake into the trees.

'Look, I'm sorry about Giles. You can have some of my cheese if I can have some of that bread?' Wil turned round. Gisella Fairfax was looking down at his hands. The bread! He had crushed one end in his fist. Gisella grinned. 'Unless you're going to hit Giles with it, that is?'

Chapter Fourteen

The Moon Chase

The hounds had been fed and were now resting. Mortimer drew his sword and in the flickering firelight marked out a small circle in the dirt.

'Right, we're here, not far from Thesker Pyke,' he said pointing his sword at the edge of the circle. 'And Skelmer Hollow is here.' He pointed to the other side of the circle. 'Over here is Dead Man's Beck, and that's Brom's Lair, just there.'

'So, we drive the wolves into Brom's Lair!' said Giles. But Mortimer shook his head.

'No. The Beck's too wide to cross there, Giles. And anyway, Wraithe Wolves hate the water; we'd never get them near. You should know that.'

Mortimer studied the map. After a few moments he seemed to make a decision.

'No. Waller, MacPhee, Lum and Drews will come with me. We'll go up here between the Pyke and Tel Harion. Deer were taken from there this morning. The best place for the Bearers is along here.' He pointed his sword to the western half of the Hollow, nearest to

Dead Man's Beck.

Gisella circled the spot with a stick. 'Okay. But the rocks on that side are easy to climb. That bank collapsed last winter, remember?' she said. 'The wolves could climb out here.'

'Hmm, good point, Fairfax. I'd forgotten about that,' frowned Mortimer.

'One of us could stand there with a burning torch?' Leon suggested. 'Wraithe Wolves absolutely hate fire. That would stop them.'

In the firelight Wil could see that everyone except for Giles was listening. Giles was throwing stones into the darkness. Mortimer nodded.

'Good idea. It's dangerous though.'

Giles was suddenly interested again. 'Oh! I know just the person for that job! Wil Calloway here, he can do it! I'll even lend him my spare crossbow and give him a couple of bolts so he can defend himself.'

Gisella did not look happy but Leon nodded.

'I think it's a good idea,' he said still studying the map. 'We need to be where we can get the best shot; if a wolf gets onto those rocks it'll be too late. Anyway Calloway's supposed to join in. And he might be lucky and stop it before it gets away!'

'And if he's not lucky?' said Gisella.

Mortimer leant forward with his elbows on his

knees; his eyes flickered gold and red as he looked into the flames.

'That's what this trial's all about, Giz.'

The plan was agreed and everyone stood waiting. Mortimer, holding a burning torch in one hand, led his horse forward.

'Right, Waller and Lum follow me. Do you all have your whistles?'

Everyone nodded except Wil. Mortimer continued.

'Remember, two short blasts if you see a wolf; two long blasts when you kill it and one long hard blast if you're in trouble.'

Everyone nodded again except Wil.

'Savidge, Beck and Fairfax, keep your bows loaded and ready. Shoot as soon as you can.'

Then he turned and gave his torch to Wil, who was standing a little way from the group, desperately hoping that they had forgotten about him. But they hadn't.

'Calloway, take this. Follow the Bearers. Leon will tell you what to do, okay Leon?' Leon gave a single nod. 'When you hear the whistle, get ready. Okay?'

He didn't wait for Wil to answer. He got on his horse to go. Then he stopped.

'By the way,' he said looking back at Wil. 'You can use a crossbow, can't you?'

'Just about!' answered Wil. Back at home he'd always preferred a broadsword, like Mortimer's, or a throwing knife. Somehow Lady Élanor or Tally knew this because he had found a short hunting knife in his pack. Luckily Giles hadn't found it when he raided the pack earlier. Just knowing the knife was now tucked into his belt made Wil feel a whole lot better.

Finally everyone was ready. The Fellhounds seemed to know something was about to happen but, try as he might[45], Wil could not read their minds.

'Well, good luck everyone,' said Mortimer, checking his saddle. He looked at the sky – the moons were hidden behind more clouds. 'Let's get these brutes long before the sun rises and get home in time for breakfast!'

As if in answer, a terrifying howl came out of the blackness – Mortimer's dark eyes twinkled.

'Okay, everyone. Let's go on a Moon Chase!'

Wil stood with the three Bearers, Leon, Giles and Gisella and watched the Chasers gallop into the darkness. His stomach tightened. At that moment Thesk's two moons appeared from behind a cloud and the lonely hills shone in their silver light.

A flapping sound made them all look up. *Pricilla!* Wil thought. But Giles swore loudly.

'Damned eagards! Come on!'

But Gisella didn't move.

'Hang on, Giles. You haven't given Wil your spare bow or any bolts.'

'Oops! I clean forgot![46]' Giles said, slapping his own forehead. 'D'you know... now I come the think, I don't think I brought it with me!'

He turned to go. Wil heard a click.

'Giles, unless you get your spare crossbow *now* I will shoot you with mine!'

Giles stopped and turned. The bolt in Gisella's crossbow was aimed at Giles's knee.

'Hang on, Fairfax! I was only joking!' said Giles, and with a slightly high-pitched laugh he walked to his pack and pulled out a second bow which he thrust towards Wil. Wil took it but kept his eyes on Gisella. Gisella held her aim. Wil held his breath.

'*And* some bolts, Giles!'

Leon stepped forward.

'Its okay, Gisella, he can have some of mine.' He was already holding out a handful of bolts. 'Here, have four – I've still got plenty.'

At last Gisella lowered her bow. But Giles went back to Mortimer's map and, using the tip of one of his bolts, he drew the shape of a skull over Dead Man's Beck. Then he walked back very close past her and stopped.

'Just be careful when I'm aiming for the wolf, Fairfax,' he hissed. *'I might miss!'*

They got to Skelmer Hollow a lot quicker than Wil had expected. In a way this was good because no one had spoken since they'd left the camp. Wil was already really worried about fighting a Wraithe Wolf, now he was worrying that he might have to stop the hunters from killing each other!

Suddenly, two short whistle blasts broke the sulky silence but it was Giles who took control.

'Get into your positions. Fairfax, down there, quick! Beck, over to the other side. Stay about half way between me and Fairfax.'

Without a word Leon and Gisella disappeared. Giles did not move. He held out his burning torch.

'Calloway, take this. Up there, on those rocks.'

Wil already had the torch Mortimer had given him but he took the one Giles offered. Clutching both torches, the crossbow and the bolts, he took a step.

'Wait!' ordered Giles and snatched the bolts from Wil's hand. With a sneer, he put three of them into the pocket of his own jacket and slid the last under Wil's arm. 'You'll only need one of those. If you miss you'll be dead!'

Then, with a cruel laugh he, too, jogged off into the night.

Wil was so angry he could hardly breathe. Struggling to hold back tears of frustration he stumbled across fallen rocks and boulders the size of Fellhounds, all piled one on top of the other. Every rock was covered in thick moss; the cloak Tally had given him was much too big; and he was trying not to drop the torches, Giles's bow or his one precious bolt.

After his third slip Wil decided he had to leave something behind or fall to his death; so he jammed one of torches between two big boulders. This made things a lot easier.

Another two short whistle blasts screamed out of the darkness but the moons had gone behind the clouds again and all Wil could see was blackness.

By the time he reached a huge, flat boulder that made an ideal lookout spot he was out of breath and sweating. He wedged the second torch between two rocks and, trying not to look down, loaded the crossbow. Then he waited, alone in the dark.

Wil wasn't sure if he'd fallen asleep and had a dream but he knew a wolf was coming along the edge of Thesker Fell. He couldn't hear or see it but he knew it was moving very slowly... and there was something soft and warm in its mouth... something that was trying to get away. Wil could feel a heart beating in terror; he could feel the wolf's heart, also beating fast – with excitement.

Images of tearing flesh and crushing bones filled Wil's head. His fingers tingled and his veins felt as though they were going to explode. Excitement filled his body. All he wanted to do was kill something – chase it, catch it and kill it. An awful taste filled Wil's mouth. The wolf swallowed. Wil retched[47]. The image went.

Wil was shaking uncontrollably[48]; his forehead burned[49]. The Wraithe Wolf had killed because it could – it enjoyed it. Wil had been scared before – now he was terrified.

Two more short whistle-blasts echoed around the rocks. The moons were also lighting up the Hollow again. Wil could see two riders and three hounds at the entrance where he knew Giles and Leon would be waiting. But he couldn't see anyone else. As he squinted into the darkness the most awful smell filled Wil's nose.

A dark shadow moved over the rocks below him and long claws scraped across the stones. Wil knew it wasn't a Fellman. As he watched, the wolf stepped into the light of the torch he had jammed in the rocks at the start of his climb. It backed away, slipped and jumped down on to the path.

Wil really didn't want to read the mind of the animal below him so he concentrated on Gisella, although he had no idea where she was. The wolf didn't move; it seemed to be watching something...

or someone. Then Wil realised... the wolf was watching Gisella! Peep, peep! Two short whistle blasts. Had Gisella seen the wolf? He waited.

The sound of Fellhounds barking, Fellmen shouting and horses snorting came from up on the Fell; the Moon Chase had started.

But below, the wolf in the hollow didn't seem to notice. Wil knew now – it was definitely watching Gisella. She was climbing down the rocks right into the wolf's path. Wil wanted to shout out. But what if that wasn't her whistle? Had she seen the wolf? What if she hadn't even seen the wolf?

The wolf took a step closer...

Wil couldn't just watch any longer, he had to do something. He clambered down the first few rocks, fell down the rest onto the path and ducked behind a dead tree. Up ahead, the wolf growled. Wil remembered the three heads hanging in the Great Hall – each one had two sets of deadly-sharp teeth!

Wil counted to three and quickly looked from behind the rotting stump. He froze.

Gisella was standing at the end of the Hollow; once again eyes fixed, feet apart and her shoulders square. This time her crossbow was aimed directly at a massive, snarling wolf that was getting ready to spring. Its hackles[50] were standing in a ridge along its back from its ears to its great, black tail, which it was wagging in slow sweeps across the ground.

But Wil's sudden movement made Gisella look up. The wolf sprang.

'*GISELLA!*' Wil screamed, and pelted forward...

'*I cannot believe you just did that!*' shouted Gisella. 'I have *never*, in my *entire* life, *ever* seen anything so stupid, *so dangerous!* You could have got me killed! And what would you have done if the wolf had turned on you – *tell me that?*'

'I would have shot it,' said Wil. He was surprised that Gisella was so cross.

'*What with?*' demanded Gisella.

It was only then that Wil realised he had left the crossbow and his one precious bolt somewhere up in the rocks.

The dead wolf lay between them. It smelt terrible. Gisella's bolt was sticking out of its chest.

'But I thought you were in trouble,' mumbled Wil. Gisella's expression suggested that she was seriously considering shooting him next! But instead she kicked the wolf's dead body and blew two very long blasts on her whistle.

'I am trained to do this, Wil. You're not!'

Luckily for Wil the sound of a horse coming their way at full gallop stopped the discussion. Mortimer's horse skidded to a halt.

'Whoa! Well done you two!' beamed Mortimer.

Mortimer's hound bounded out of the darkness and stood beside him panting.

'Yeah, thanks – lucky shot!' said Gisella without looking at Wil. 'Any more out there?'

'Oh yes! Tarek and Cali tried to bring one down just now but he got away in the rocks. Y' know, I could understand if they were killing for food, but we found *fourteen* dead deer up there. I swear they just enjoy killing!'

Wil said nothing.

'Right, well, I'll take this out of the way and we'll see what else we can bring down for you!' said Mortimer. He threw a rope to Gisella who tied it around the wolf's neck. Mortimer kicked his horse into a walk and dragged the filthy body out of Skelmer Hollow and away into the night. Wil turned to Gisella.

'Thanks.'

'For what!' Gisella was still cross.

'For not telling Mortimer about the crossbow.'

She stood in the darkness and looked straight at him.

'Look, this is your trial. If you die that proves you're guilty. I'd prefer it if you lived and proved that you're innocent; I'd also prefer that none of us get killed in the process[51]! Now, I suggest you go find your crossbow – you might need it next time!'

The moons appeared and helpfully lit up the mossy stones as Wil re-traced his steps across the skids and scrapes he'd made on the boulders on his way down. He had to find the crossbow. There was no way he was going to tell Giles he'd lost it.

He slipped on a rock. Godwyn Savidge's announcement at the festival came back to him, *"killed or injured"*; if Wil went back to Saran injured that would also prove his guilt.

But, as Wil moved to get up, his fingers touched the wooden shaft of Giles's crossbow. It was still loaded! It was, however, stuck in the rocks. Before he kicked it loose he carefully released the bolt and slid it down into his boot for safe keeping.

Back up on the wide ledge Wil sat with his back once again firmly against solid stone. He could see both ends of the Hollow, but it was only now that he had stopped groaning, swearing, slipping and stomping that Wil noticed it had gone quiet – like someone had thrown a heavy blanket over the landscape. The hairs on his neck stood up and goose bumps prickled up his arms.

A long, loud whistle blasted out of the silence. Wil waited for the second blast. It didn't come. Mortimer had said one long blast meant trouble–

'*NO, GILES. GET BACK DOWN! GILES – NOOOOOO!*'

Terrible sounds of snarling and gnashing[52] mixed with the terrified screams of a young man. Then a single blood-chilling howl and a whistle-blast that seemed to go on and on forever.

One of the moons inched around a cloud as if it was trying to see what had happened. Wil was desperate to get up onto the Fell as quickly as possible. He stepped backwards to look for a way up the sheer rock above him and felt his heel kick Giles's bow. The sound of the crossbow tumbling down onto the rocks below told Wil that, this time, his chance to shoot anything with it had *definitely* been lost.

Then two short whistle blasts sounded again and Wil heard Gisella.

'Wil, down here – down here, *they're coming!* Bring the bow and get down here now!'

With the silver-tipped bolt now safe in his boot, Wil charged down towards Gisella. He jumped from boulder to boulder – almost flying down the steep slope. For Wil, at this moment, heights were *not* a problem!

'What do you mean – *they*?' Wil panted as he landed at Gisella's side.

'There are two of them!' she whispered, pointing her bow slightly to the left. There, in the rocks, right at the end of the narrow gully, crouched a massive Wraithe Wolf. Its belly was almost touching the ground as it inched towards them. Even at that distance Wil could smell its acrid stench[53]. Huge fangs jutted down from either side of its terrifying jaws – they were dripping with something black.

'Aim for its chest, Wil. One bolt right through the–... Wil... where's your crossbow?'

The forced calm in Gisella's voice took Wil by surprise.

'I'll explain later, Gisella – but I've got this.'

She glanced down at the hunting knife that he had just pulled from his belt but at the same moment, the nightmare got worse.

Silhouetted against one of the moons, a four-legged shape scrambled over the rocks right where Wil had just been sitting. It jumped and joined the stalking wolf ahead of them.

'I said there were two,' said Gisella.

The wolves crawled along the narrow floor of Skelmer Hollow. Wil could hear the sound of running water behind them and guessed they were near Dead Man's Beck.

'Wil, whatever you do, don't turn and run; I can kill one of them but one of us will be dead before I can re-load,' said Gisella calmly.

Wil had an idea.

'If I can get close enough, I'm pretty sure I can hit one of them with my knife.'

There was a very short 'Peep!' behind them.

'Giles... Leon... is that you?' Gisella sounded utterly relieved but she kept her eyes fixed on the wolves in front of her.

'It's Leon.'

The young Bearer's voice sounded husky and tired.

'You okay, Leon? Where's Giles?'

'He's... he's back there, Giz. Mortimer and Olivia are... er... there. Between the three of us we should be able to stop these two from going up the side.'

'It's okay, Leon, I don't think they're planning to make a run for it,' whispered Gisella. 'But it's alright 'cos our friend here has brought his knife!'

'Knife? But he had Giles's spare bow?' said Leon.

Wil cringed.

'Look, I dropped it, okay! Not great, but I'll do my best with what I've got and if the wolf gets me – well, there we go – guilty as charged!'

The blade of Wil's hunting knife glinted in the moonlight.

'Well, it looks sharp enough,' said Leon kindly.

Wil heard Gisella take a swift breath as if she was going to deliver another stinging attack but at that moment one of the wolves charged and leapt at Gisella. Wil heard a click but nothing happened. Gisella ducked. The beast went over her head and crashed straight into Leon.

Gisella screamed, '*Leon!*'

He was flat on his back. He didn't answer.

The wolf span round and dropped to the floor, haunches[54] raised ready to launch again.

'Keep your eyes on the other one!' ordered Gisella.

'What happened?' asked Wil.

'My bow jammed – it happens, I'm afraid,' she answered. 'The problem is I've got to bang it on the floor to release the nut!'

'So, we're two bows down and two Wraithe Wolves still standing,' said Wil dryly.

Gisella ignored his sarcasm.

'I need to get to Leon's bow, Wil. It's our only chance.'

Leon's loaded crossbow was only about an arm's length from Gisella – if she was very careful, very quick – *and very lucky* – she should be able to reach it. Then Wil

126

remembered the bolt in his boot.

'Hang on Gisella.'

Trying not to make any sudden movements Wil tucked his knife back into his belt and pulled the bolt from his boot.

'After three, drop down and go for the bow, okay?'

'Wil, I can do this on my own. You don't have to– '

'*Just do it, will you!*' begged Wil. 'If we both get out of this alive you can give me a lecture later!'

She blinked at him but said nothing.

'On three. One… Two… '

He held the silver tip of the bolt behind his head and yelled, '*THREEEE!*'

Surprised by the sudden noise, the wolf behind them hesitated. Wil hurled the bolt with every ounce of strength he had in his body and closed his eyes.

'Well, blow me!' said Gisella. 'You got 'im!'

Wil opened his eyes. But before he had time to admire his handiwork the sound of long claws scrabbling[55] over loose gravel made them both turn round – the second wolf was charging towards them. Gisella leapt for Leon's bow. Wil wrenched the knife from his belt. The wolf leapt…

Wil knew the beast was dead but as it flew past his ear one of its barbed claws caught his shoulder. It tore into the thick wool of his cloak and raked through his flesh – the pain was excruciating[56].

'Got him!' announced Gisella, standing over the second body.

Wil walked up and kicked the animal over with his boot, trying to ignore the searing[57] pain in his arm. There, sticking out of its chest was a silver-tipped crossbow bolt, split cleanly in two by a short hunting knife that was sunk into the beast's chest right up to the hilt.

'Well done!' said Wil, and fainted.

'Yes, Becky, but he *saved* Leon and me!' Gisella was saying when Wil came round.

He opened his eyes. It was still night. Both girls were looking down at him. Cali, Becky's Fellhound, was lying a little way off, panting heavily. Sprawled out next to Wil were the carcasses of two dead Wraithe Wolves. The stench was overpowering.

'But you heard what the Order said, Gisella – killed *or injured*. I can't see *that* getting better by morning, can you? Look at all that blood! Anyway, he's not the one we need to be worrying about at the moment!'

'Yes,' said Gisella. 'Leon's still out cold – look at that bruise! Can you take him back to the camp on– '

Something made Gisella stop talking for a moment.

'You weren't talking about Leon were you, Becky?'

'No, Giz. It's... ' Becky stopped and turned away. Then the words tumbled out of her mouth. 'They got Giles, Gizzy. *He just wouldn't listen!* He came up onto the Fell – he got between Olivia and Sharus. Mortimer tried... oh, Gizzy – it was *awful.'*

She started to sob. Wil struggled to his feet. Tears were streaming down the Chaser's grubby face. Cali was at her side in a second.

'I know you didn't really like him, Gizzy, but – oh, I wouldn't wish that on *anyone,*' Becky sobbed.

'Has he... been taken?' Gisella asked quietly.

'Yes – it was horrible. Once he'd.., uh... ch-changed he let out the most awful howl and then galloped away into the darkness. Since then Mortimer's been trying to get Olivia to come away but she won't leave the spot where he fell.'

Gisella gave Becky a hug and then frowned down at the dead wolves.

'Look Becky, I know it sounds heartless but we really need to get these two up onto Tel Harion before dawn.' Then she added, almost to herself. 'If we don't, *we're all going to be in trouble!'*

CHAPTER FIFTEEN

Wraithe Wolves

Olivia's voice drifted over the hillside as they approached the fire. She spoke with no emotion at all. Her horse lay dead just feet from where she sat.

'We were going to get married. He promised me. After my eighteenth birthday, next summer. I told my mother. What am I going to do now?'

A tear rolled down her cheek.

'I don't think you ought to think too much about that now, Livy,' said Mortimer. His arm was around her shoulder – he'd been crying, too. 'Come back to the camp, hey?'

Curtis threw another branch into the crackling flames and raised an approving eyebrow at the body of the wolf dragging behind Becky's horse. Leon was flopped over the saddle, still unconscious.

'How many did you get?' Curtis asked Gisella.

'Three. There's one still down in the Hollow,' said Gisella. 'Mortimer, it's nearly dawn. Where's the one you took earlier? We need to get them on the fire.'

In the distance, to the east, the horizon glowed with

a hint of burnt amber. Both moons had waned[58] a while ago. Dawn was indeed on its way.

'Just give us a minute, Giz,' said Mortimer. 'He's not far from that crop of pines over there. Can you, Wil and Curtis go?'

He pointed down towards a distant copse[59] of dark trees.

'Okay, but you and Becky need to get the other one – really Mort, we're running out of time.' Gisella's insistent tone made Olivia look up.

'You never liked him, did you, Gisella?'

Becky stepped forward and put her hand up to stop Gisella from answering.

'Not now, Liv.'

'But she didn't!' Olivia insisted with a strange laugh. 'You *never* believed his story did you, Gisella? You just wouldn't believe that he was brave and capable. He should have been a Chaser. But you – always disagreeing with him or criticising him. You did your best to turn Mortimer against him!'

Olivia was on her feet now. Mortimer's bloodshot eyes darted between both girls. Curtis went over to stoke the fire and Becky started to cry again. Emmet and Wil looked away, embarrassed.

'I don't really know what you're talking about Olivia. Look, we need to burn the bodies before dawn. You know what'll happen if we don't, don't you?' Wil could see that Gisella was doing her best to stay calm. She moved to put her hand on Olivia's arm.

'Don't touch me!' spat Olivia. She jerked away. 'I hate you! It was because of you he tried so hard. This was his idea. He was going to show you all!'

Olivia dropped to the ground and sobbed. Sharus limped over and flopped down beside her. Wil could see that the hound's hind quarter was ripped open and the lower half of his left ear was missing. Mortimer was looking desperate now.

'Emmet, can you take Olivia back to the camp on Minstrel?'

Emmet ran his hand down both of his horse's front legs; Wil could see one leg was swollen.

'Er, I don't think so, Mort, he's lame[60].'

'Right, well take Shadow as well,' said Mortimer, handing the reins of his own horse to Emmet. Leon moaned quietly, although he did look a little steadier on Becky's horse.

'Take Leon, Becky, and go with Emmet. We'll burn the bodies and see you all back at the camp. If we leave it much longer we won't just have *dead* Wraithe Wolves to worry about!'

'You sure about this, Mort?' asked Emmet.

'Yes,' said Mortimer and he scooped Olivia into his arms and put her on Minstrel's back. She didn't resist[61].

Becky climbed up behind Emmet.

'D'you think Giles suffered, Mortimer? Could he feel himself changing… you know… into a…' She stopped and took a deep breath. 'Wil, I think you'd better have these.' She held out a handful of bolts. 'They're Leon's but somehow I don't think he'll need them.' Then she called their hounds and Emmet turned Shadow away.

Mortimer grabbed hold of Tarek's collar to stop him from following the others.

'Right,' he said. 'Let's get these bodies on the fire and go home!'

The smell of burning Wraithe Wolves and the pain from his shoulder were almost too much for Wil but he pushed on[62], desperate not to show that he was hurt.

As they put the second body on the fire Mortimer made a suggestion.

'Look Gisella, if you and Wil stay here to make sure that those two don't fall off the fire, or put it out, Curtis and I'll go down and get the last one.'

He looked exhausted; his face black with smoke and smut from the burning bodies.

'Okay. But you're going to have to fly. The sun's going to be up any minute.' Gisella answered looking at the horizon.

Curtis jumped back on to his horse and held his arm

down. 'We're probably a bit heavy for Blaze, but over this distance he'll be fine. Stella, Tarek, come.'

Wil and Gisella watched the two Fellmen and their hounds disappear into a dip, a long howl rose from the hills above them. Suddenly Tel Harion felt every bit as bleak and lonely as Lady Élanor had first described it.

Gisella grabbed her crossbow and handed Leon's to Wil. Her mouth was smiling but her eyes were telling a different story altogether. 'How's your arm, Wil?'

'It's fine. Fine, yeah… *argh!*'

He couldn't say anything else. Rage and hate suddenly engulfed[63] him. Images of tearing flesh and splattering gore[64] filled his mind – the smell of blood in his nostrils was completely overwhelming. He dropped to his knees and vomited[65].

'Wil, what's wrong?' Gisella screamed. Then he heard her hastily loading her crossbow and her voice went deathly calm. 'They're here, Wil – they've come for their dead!'

'I know,' croaked Wil. Sweat poured down his temple. His arm no longer hurt; the desire to kill was overwhelming. With a huge effort he held on to Leon's bow and the bolts, and grabbed Gisella's arm.

'We've got to get out of here – *NOW!*'

Yelling the last word, he forced the images out of his mind and pulled Gisella after him. Leaping over gullies and crevices, they pelted down the steep hillside.

'We've got to get to the Hollow to warn the others!' cried Gisella.

'*I think they might already know!*' Wil shouted back.

In seconds they were at the entrance to Skelmer Hollow where Curtis and Mortimer were waiting for them. Blaze danced around, while Stella and Tarek prowled up and down restlessly, barking at every new howl.

'I don't think we're going to be able to get that last body up to the fire, Mortimer,' panted Gisella. Behind her there was no sign of any movement up on the Fell, but the howling was *definitely* getting nearer.

'Sounds like they're about two leagues away,' said Mortimer, listening intently.

'*They?*' Wil blurted out.

'Oh, yes, Wil. The last time this happened was when the Fellmen of Saran took the bodies of three dead Wraithe Wolves as trophies[66] – Saran was attacked by the whole pack! We lost Fellmen, hounds and horses that day.'

'We don't really know why but if we burn the bodies on the Fell before dawn, the wolves leave us alone – odd but true,' said Curtis with a shrug.

'So why did you keep the heads – in the Great Hall?' asked Wil.

'In memory of those who fell – and as a reminder

of the grave mistake that was made on that Moon Chase,' answered Mortimer.

Another howl ripped through the air – this time much nearer. Blaze reared.

'Curtis, take Stella. Go help the others,' ordered Mortimer. 'Don't wait for us. We'll try to give you a bit more time.'

'Not quite sure how we're going to do that, Mortimer,' said Gisella. She was looking scared now.

Mortimer nodded towards the huge mound of stinking black fur that lay sprawled across the path.

'We've still got your dead friend down there, haven't we?'

With the sound of galloping hooves fading into the distance, Wil, Gisella and Mortimer ran to the dead wolf.

'Wow!' said Mortimer looking at the bolt, split into two by a hunting knife sticking out of the creature's chest.

'That was Wil. He's pretty good with a blade – luckily!'

Mortimer wrenched the knife out of the deadly wound and held it out.

'Well, in that case,' he said to Wil, 'you'd better have it back!'

Wil took the knife gratefully but the seething anger[67] of the approaching Wraithe Wolves was creeping over him again. He had no idea how many wolves there were but he knew that they were coming fast.

He looked down the gully and tried to remember Mortimer's map.

'What's down there?' he asked.

'Dead Man's Beck,' answered Mortimer. He and Gisella were frantically[68] tying a rope to the slain[69] wolf's legs ready to haul it back up towards the entrance of the Hollow.

Wil scanned the rock-fall. The ledge where he had been perched earlier that night didn't seem nearly as high in the day light.

'Wait!' he said as something dawned on him. 'If we bring the wolves in this far up they'll be able to come in behind us. We'll be trapped!'

'Whatever you're thinking Wil, say it. We really haven't got much time!' Wil could hear the desperation in Mortimer's voice. He went on quickly.

'We need to get into the narrow part of the Hollow so they can't come at us from too many directions. I don't suppose you, er, picked up Giles's bow, did you?' he felt awkward but had to ask. Mortimer turned out his pockets and looked back at Wil.

'That'll be "No" then,' said Wil flatly. 'Okay. Gisella, how many bolts have you got left?'

'Um... nine... ten... twelve,' she said after a rapid count.

'And Becky gave me six – so that's eighteen between us,' said Wil.

He handed Leon's bow and three of the bolts to Mortimer.

'Take this… and these. Gisella, can you spare any?'

'Here,' she said and handed Mortimer four of her own precious bolts. 'Wil?'

'Without two good arms,' he said looking directly at Gisella, 'I figure you two'll be better off with the bows. Don't worry about me, I'll think of something.'

Mortimer's confused expression turned to horrified realisation.

'Two good arms? Wil, you're not injured – *are you?*'

But a piercing howl from the entrance to the Hollow saved Wil from answering.

Tarek dropped flat to the ground and growled. Gisella and Mortimer loaded their crossbows.

'I think they've found us,' breathed Gisella.

CHAPTER SIXTEEN

Trapped

Two Wraithe Wolves were standing on the moss covered rocks, saliva dripping from their panting jaws.

'We've got to get further back. If those two get behind us we won't stand a chance – especially if they bring their friends!' shouted Wil. But Mortimer didn't agree. Another black, snarling shape was creeping towards them along the path, body low, ears pricked forward.

'No! You two – go! Tarek and I'll tackle this one,' he insisted, nodding down the path away from the beck.

'No, we need to stick together,' Wil insisted. 'We can do this if we work like them – *in a pack!* Start moving backwards – slowly. Keep your eyes on him, Mortimer. Gisella, watch those two. I'll keep a look out for any others. We need to get to that gap.'

'I really don't think the Beck's a good idea, Wil,' said Mortimer. But the sound of falling rocks made them all look up – the two wolves were no longer standing at the top of the slope.

'Quick, head for that tree stump!' cried Wil, trying to remind himself to breathe.

All three of them backed-up[70] hastily. Tarek's amber eyes watched Mortimer, waiting for a command. As they reached the moss-coated stump Mortimer said quietly, 'Drop!'

Tarek obeyed immediately.

'Watch,' said Mortimer and pointed. Tarek fixed his gaze on the advancing wolf.

With one wolf on the path and the other two balanced expertly on a boulder above them they were now in real danger of being surrounded. Drool dripped off their yellow fangs – they really did look like they were smiling. Wil could feel no fear in them – in fact, all he was feeling at that moment was pleasure.

'*They're enjoying this!*' he thought.

Suddenly, the lone[71] wolf launched forwards towards them.

Wil heard Mortimer's quiet voice, 'Waaiit, Tarek, Waaiit... *NOW – GO!*'

Tarek leapt into the wolf's path and stopped. The wolf skidded to a halt and lowered its head. Wil was terrified and fascinated[72] at the same time – the two wolves on the rocks watched. Mortimer took aim and Gisella stepped in front of Wil with her bow up. Everyone held their breath.

Then, from the top of Skelmer Hollow, a boy's

voice called out.

'Mortimer? Gisella… Are you there?'

'What the…?'

But Mortimer didn't get the chance to finish. All three wolves saw the opportunity and charged.

Tarek sprang – hound and wolf crashed together – their jaws locked in combat[73]. Mortimer tried desperately to aim his bow so that he could get one good shot at the wolf, but the two animals were fighting too furiously.

As the fight on the ground raged, the other two wolves careered down from the rocks to join in. Gisella's first shot felled[74] the leader before he hit the path. But in the time it took her to re-load, the second was almost on them.

'Duck!' shouted Wil and pushed Gisella out of the way. He launched one of his bolts. It went straight into the wolf's open mouth and embedded into the back of its throat.

Choking and writhing[75], the creature tried to shake the bolt free, but it was stuck fast. A second bolt thwacked[76] into its chest and finally it slumped to the ground, dead.

The noise from the fighting hound and wolf was terrible. Snarls and gnashes mixed with agonised howls – it was clear to Wil that neither was going to give up.

'I can't get a shot,' Mortimer shouted. 'I don't know how much more he can take!'

They all watched, utterly helpless, while Tarek fought the battle of his life. The Wraithe Wolf wasn't as big as the Fellhound but it had the advantage of long, deadly fangs, two sets of teeth and vicious, barbed claws – just like the one that had cut into Wil's shoulder earlier.

Then a movement to Wil's left – two more Wraithe Wolves dropped down to join the fight. Like waves crashing onto rocks, the beasts hurtled[77] towards them and leapt.

Wil ducked, closed his eyes and thrust his knife upwards above his head as hard as he could with both hands. The pain down his arm was terrible, but he ignored it. Warm blood splattered over him and an agonised howl told Wil his blade had done its job. But as he wiped his eyes he could see Gisella on the ground.

'Gisella!' His breath caught in his throat. But then, to his relief, she rolled over. Her crossbow was still loaded. She looked past Wil and fired. A bolt whistled past Wil's ear and he heard a dull thud behind him. Gisella's expression told him she'd hit her target. The Hollow was quiet.

'That was close!'

'Yes, he bowled me over[78], but I'm OK,' she said smiling at him.

'I meant your bolt!'

'Oh, that – Oh, I knew I'd miss you!' Gisella got

to her feet looking very pleased with herself. 'Where's Mortimer?'

A yell of pure anger filled the Hollow. Mortimer was marching away from them, loading, shooting and reloading his crossbow. Firing one bolt after another – *thunk, thunk, thunk!*

'Oh no,' Gisella went white. 'Not Tarek!'

Past Mortimer, in the direction he was headed, Wil could see two bodies lying flat out on the ground. Mortimer reached Tarek and fired one final bolt into the already well and truly dead wolf. Then he dropped to the floor and laid his hands on the neck of his dead friend. By the time Wil and Gisella reached him he was weeping silently and stroking Tarek's blood-soaked coat.

Wil couldn't think of anything to say and, by the look on her face, neither could Gisella. But the one question that burned in Wil's mind was: who had shouted?

Then the sound of footsteps running towards them brought the answer. There, pelting down the path, followed closely by a huge Fellhound, was Seth Tanner. He was smiling broadly.

'There you are – I've been looking for... Oh... Mortimer... oh!'

Seth's smile disappeared. Mortimer spoke through gritted teeth.

'What in the name of all that is good brings you here, Seth Tanner?'

Suddenly on his feet, Mortimer's blood-drenched hands were clutching Seth's throat. Farrow was barking loudly. Wil could feel her confusion – she knew Mortimer.

'What were you thinking, you *stupid* boy! This is your fault – *TAREK IS DEAD AND IT'S YOUR FAULT!*'

Wil and Gisella managed to free Seth before Mortimer finished him off. The young boy backed away towards Farrow, rubbing his neck and coughing. Wil kept a firm grip on Mortimer while Gisella stood in front of Seth. Once Seth could breathe he started to gabble.

'I saw Curtis… he said you were in trouble. I gave him my horse, er… you know, Roani, …my father, er… doesn't, hum, know I'm here, um…'

'*You what?*' Mortimer was livid. With his face still wet with tears, he paced up and down, obviously trying to stop himself from attacking the boy again. 'What do you mean – *he doesn't know you're here?*'

While they waited for an explanation, Wil glanced towards Tel Harion. The hillside was covered with specks of black – all moving towards the Hollow – *very* quickly.

'Mortimer,' said Wil with a calm he did not feel.

'No, Wil. I really want to hear what this idiot thinks he was up to!'

Wil watched the specks getting bigger by the second.

'Uh, Mort, mate, I *really* think you should have a look at this,' insisted Wil.

Irritated, Mortimer span round and followed Wil's pointing finger.

'RUN!' he yelled. Grabbing Seth's arm he headed for the narrow gap in the rocks that led to Dead Man's Beck. The others, including Farrow, followed close behind.

No-one dared to look back as they ducked through the gap and stopped dead – just in time.

'Oh great!' said Wil as he tried not to look down. A long, narrow ledge spread out on either side of them. Below – quite a long way below – was a glistening green pool flowing into a series of long rapids. To their left, the ledge ended abruptly; to their right the ledge narrowed into a path that seemed to lead back up onto the Fell.

Seth immediately turned and headed up the path, but Farrow let out a single warning bark.

'Oh, come on girl,' he said, turning back to her. 'It's the only way out!'

'It's also the way in!' said Gisella flatly. 'Seth, on three, I need you to drop to your knees.'

'Now look, I'm not begging anyone for anything!' Seth glared at her. Behind him a Wraithe Wolf crept around the bend into his path. Gisella raised her crossbow.

'*THREE!*' she yelled and fired – the boy dropped to the ground just in time.

The wolf wobbled for a moment and for one horrendous[79] second Wil thought Gisella had missed. But then it toppled sideways off the ledge. A full second later there was a distant splash.

'I don't think that way is going to get us out of trouble,' said Gisella, loading her bow automatically without taking her eyes off the path. Her statement was confirmed by a deep growl.

'There's only one way to go,' announced Mortimer. 'For those who want to live – JUMP NOW!'

Mortimer ran forward, kicked himself off the ledge and disappeared.

As the growling snarl grew louder Wil, Gisella and Seth looked at each other.

'Come on,' said Wil. 'You too, Farrow!'

Wil plunged[80] into the icy water. His heavy cloak dragged him under but his foot kicked a rock and he was able to balance and catch his breath. To his surprise, he was still holding his knife.

Farrow was already on the opposite bank shaking herself from head to tail. There was no sign of Seth, though.

The sound of annoyed spluttering told Wil that Gisella was still alive. She was further along the bank, stumbling through the shallows towards Farrow. One leg of her breeches was soaked with bright red blood. Had the Wraithe Wolf got her just before they'd jumped?

Wil was about to shout over when he heard a groan, and a movement in the branches of a thick bush that stretched out over the pool caught his eye.

'Mortimer? Seth?' Wil called out.

The answer was another long groan, followed by a wheezing cough. Wil half swam, half paddled towards the noise as quickly as his heavy, wet clothes would let him. He could see someone suspended in the bush just above the water. It was Mortimer; he was dangling across a thick branch and the branches above him were all snapped and battered.

'Gisella, over here – it's Mortimer. He's in the bush – I think he's injured.' Wil called out. 'Mortimer… Mort… Are you okay?'

'Urgh, yer... I think I am, but... can't breathe too well... huruhh,' panted Mortimer. 'Something's stopping me... from getting... uhh... freeee...'

Through the tangle of branches Wil could see that Mortimer's cloak was wound around a branch. He was stuck.

'Mortimer, are you alright?' Gisella called from the other bank. She waded back into the ice-cold water and with graceful strokes pulled herself quickly through the water. Wil watched in admiration[81] – his swimming style was far more splash than speed!

With Gisella's help Wil managed to cut the knotted cloak and Mortimer dropped with a splash. He came back to the surface and spat out a mouthful of water.

'My ribs hurt like hell, but at least I *was* dry!'

The three of them were heading for the nearest bank when Farrow's deep bark stopped them in their tracks.

'Oh no, Seth!' shouted Wil. Just in front of the Fellhound, heading for the rapids, Seth was thrashing and gasping.

'I... can't... sw...' and then he disappeared under the water.

Farrow barked and barked. Wil stumbled across the rocks. He pulled the heavy cloak over his head, dropped it, and dived towards the spot where Seth had gone under.

Wil swam down, desperately peering through the murky green – the crushing cold made his head feel like it was going to explode. Just as he thought his lungs would burst, a pale hand drifted in front of him. He grabbed it and kicked his legs with every ounce of strength he had left. He burst above the surface and gasped gulps of wonderful fresh air. Gisella was waiting.

'I'll take him, Wil.'

She grabbed Seth's white chin in her cupped hand and swam towards Farrow who was up to her chest in the water, still barking.

Mortimer waded-in, too, and dragged Wil the final few feet to the bank where he flopped on to the pebbles, absolutely exhausted.

Beside him, Gisella was doing her best to breathe life back into Seth's still frame.

'*Come ON, you stupid boy!*' she shouted and banged down hard on his chest with both fists.

A gush of water flowed out of Seth's mouth; he gasped and started coughing. Gisella burst into tears.

'Thanks,' Seth managed to croak to Gisella after a moment.

'It's not me you need to thank – *it's him!*' She pointed to Wil, who was still lying on the ground. 'Wil Calloway – *that's* who you need to thank, for saving your life!'

CHAPTER SEVENTEEN

Heading Home

They were cold and wet and the stones dug into their backs, but all four of them had fallen asleep as soon as they were all safely on the bank of the river.

Wil opened his eyes. He could smell smoke. Farrow was lying against Seth who was snoring gently; the boy looked very small against the huge hound. Farrow was dozing, but at the slightest noise she would look up – she was watching over them.

The smoke was coming from a small fire that Mortimer was feeding with twigs and sticks. The sun was shining and items of clothing were hanging over the surrounding bushes and branches – including, Wil smiled, Old Mr Barrowman's cloak.

Wil's whole body ached as he made his way across the stony bank to join Mortimer.

'Look what I found when I was hanging your cloak out,' said Mortimer, pointing to three silvery salmon cooking over the flames. The fish were skewered onto long sticks that Mortimer was carefully turning over. They smelt delicious.

'Nearly cooked – shame we haven't got any –' Mortimer didn't finish the sentence; he was staring at Wil's arm. Wil looked, too. His shirt was soaked in blood.

'I'd forgotten,' said Mortimer. 'Back there. You got injured.'

He went back to turning the fish.

'Er, oh yeah,' answered Wil. 'Good job I was wearing that cloak – could have been a lot worse, hey?'

'But the Order... they said– '

'We all know what they said, Mortimer!' Gisella was striding towards them. Her shirt was green from the slimy rocks and the right thigh of her breeches was brown with thick, dried blood. 'But do you honestly think that a guilty man would have fought so hard last night to protect us? Or cut you free back there, when he could have taken the opportunity to escape? *Or* risked his own life to save the person he was originally accused of trying to murder – *do you?*'

'Well, er... No, of course not,' said Mortimer. 'But I'm not the Order, Gisella. Godwyn Savidge and Oswald Beck may not see it that way!'

Wil noticed that Mortimer had not mentioned Gisella's own mother, Fermina, who had been equally convinced of Wil's guilt.

Gisella pressed her lips together and turned away. Wil watched her wander[82] away along the bank. She stopped by a thick bush and took off her torn, bloody trousers which she hung next to her mail shirt.

Wil, too, made his way along the water's edge. He walk past Gisella, letting the sound of flowing water dilute[83] the horrific memories of the previous night. He wondered what had happened to Giles – or rather the Wraithe Wolf that Giles had become. He couldn't stop thinking about Giles transforming into a wolf – hair erupting[84] all over his body, his jaw cracking and stretching, razor sharp teeth burrowing[85] through his gums, pushing out his human ones. Wil squeezed his eyes tight shut and shivered.

A sudden 'Crronk, Crronk, Prruk!' pushed the horrible thoughts from his mind. A big, black raven was perched on a branch and swinging from its beak was the pink silk bag!

Seeing that she had Wil's attention, Pricilla dropped the bag onto the stones, jumped down and pecked at the ribbon drawn tight across its neck until it loosened. The bag opened. Then she poked her huge beak into the bag and dragged out a smaller, blue bag. Wil could see a little label attached to one corner which Pricilla kept picking up and dropping; picking up and dropping.

'Crronk, Prruk, Prruk.'

After the fourth time, it dawned on Wil that she wanted him to read the label. He picked up the little package:

For wounds: dust on and cover for two days.
Do not swallow.
Best before: Spring's first full moon

'Lady Élanor!' Wil murmured.

'Crronk!' Pricilla nudged the larger bag towards him and then took off up into the sky, did an elegant somersault and disappeared over the cliff top high above him.

Wil turned the blue bundle over and over in his fingers and read the label again. Was Pricilla telling him to use this on his shoulder? How would he cover the wound? Everything was wet and he certainly didn't have a clean bandage!

'What've you got there?' Gisella was right behind him.

Unsure how long she had been watching he risked a lie, 'Oh, nothing!'

At the same moment he kicked the bag at his feet. A crisp white bandage rolled out onto the stones. Another label, fastened tightly around it with a piece of twine read:

For wounds: bind and do not remove for TWO days.
Do not swallow.
Best before: The crescent moons of the third quarter

Wil couldn't stop himself from laughing.

'What's that then?' said Gisella; although she was smiling, too.

'Oh, it's something that Lady Élanor and Tally made for me.'

'Didn't Giles throw something like that away when he ransacked your bag?' asked Gisella frowning at the memory.

'Na, I had this tucked in my trousers!' Wil lied again; he didn't know how much Gisella knew about Lady Élanor's raven, Pricilla.

'Look, it's a first aid kit for an idiot!' He showed her the bandage and the little blue bag. She read the labels and then peered at his shoulder.

'Well, I don't suppose it'll do any harm to cover that up; we'd better get that blood off your shirt, too. Or Seth'll start asking awkward questions!'

Wil pulled off his shirt and Gisella sprinkled the powder onto his shoulder; the pain completely disappeared as soon as the pale green dust touched the wound.

Once Gisella had secured the bandage, Wil quickly washed the blood off his shirt and pulled it back on before Seth woke up and saw the dressing. Gisella sat back. A trickle of fresh blood leaked from the neat slice in her own thigh.

'How d'you do that?' asked Wil.

'As I landed in the water... underground branch I

think. I'll be fine,' said Gisella. Blood dripped onto the stones under her leg.

Wil shook the little blue package.

'Right, well if this stuff's good enough for me, it'll be good enough for you!'

'What're you two up to?'

It was Mortimer.

'Lady Élanor gave Wil a first aid kit,' said Gisella. Mortimer eyed the green powder in Wil's cupped hand.

'Have *you* used it?' he asked, nodding towards Wil's shoulder.

'Yep, and now we're going to put some on Gisella's leg!' Wil announced and sprinkled the green dust over her wound.

Wil was just fastening the bandage when they were joined by Seth. He looked groggy and damp.

He looked at the pieces of cloth on the ground.

'Bandages? Did someone get hurt?'

Mortimer and Gisella answered at exactly the same time.

'Me!'

'Gisella!'

Seth looked at Gisella's bandaged leg and, satisfied with the answer, he turned back to Wil.

'Apparently I owe you my thanks.' Although his expression didn't suggest that he really was grateful.

'That's one way of putting it!' said Gisella, with a sniff.

'But my father – everyone – said you tried to kill me. Why did you do that… then… save me back there?' Seth waved his hand towards the water.

Although Wil heard Gisella's sharp intake of breath, Mortimer spoke first.

'You still don't get it do you, Tanner? I don't know who did try to kill you the other day but I honestly believe that this person is *not* the one!' He pointed towards Wil but kept his eyes fixed on Seth. 'I believe Wil's story – that he was trying to save you. Just like he risked his own life to save you this morning, and just like he helped us up there last night. If it wasn't for Wil, Giles Savidge wouldn't be the only one running with the Wraithe Wolves right now!'

Seth staggered back as if someone had punched him.

'Oh, No… *Giles?* You mean Giles has become a *Wraithe Wolf?*'

'Yes, Seth,' said Mortimer.

'But how? He fought one before. He came back. He was a hero.' Seth whispered the last few words almost to himself. He stumbled to the water's edge and stared blankly out over the cold, green pool.

Mortimer went after him and put his hand on the shocked boy's shoulder. 'I'm sorry Seth, but this time Giles made a mistake. He... he just wouldn't listen.'

'He never forgave Cae, you know – or Ellyn – to tell the truth, he made Cae's life a misery,' said Seth.

Wil had heard enough.

'Yes, that's because Giles Savidge was a nasty bully! He was also a liar!'

'Wil, steady on now,' said Mortimer.

'No! He lied about how he got injured!'

'Lied? What do you mean? I was there, Wil – I saw the wolf attacking him.' Mortimer didn't blink as he faced Wil.

'He wasn't bitten,' Wil insisted. 'You didn't see the wolf actually *bite him*, did you Mortimer? Giles had already been attacked by a mountain lion; the wolf was just licking his blood when you saw him!'

'How do you know, Wil?' Gisella asked.

He'd said too much. He was putting Lady Élanor and her sister in danger.

'Well... er... I'm only guessing about the lion...' he blustered[86]. 'But I don't believe Giles was attacked by a Wraithe Wolf that time. Think about it. He got attacked last night and turned into a wolf immediately, didn't he?'

His three companions looked at him in shocked silence. Wil turned away and stomped back to the fire.

'I think these fish are cooked!'

They ate in silence, each lost in their own thoughts. When she had finished, Gisella, licking her fingers, went down to the water's edge and splashed her hands into a shallow pool. Wil followed.

'Do you think I'm going to get out of this?' he asked.

A rainbow slick[87] of salmon oil drifted among the rocks and away down stream.

'To be honest Wil, I don't know. If Seth believes you... well maybe he can convince the Order you're innocent. You've certainly convinced Mortimer and me.'

'But my shoulder – Giles's father said if I returned injured I would hang as that proves I'm guilty.'

She put her hand lightly on his good arm and smiled.

'Well then, we just won't tell them you got injured!'

With the meal finished, Mortimer began to get restless. He wasn't at all happy about staying so close to Tel Harion for a second night. Seth complained he was too tired and hadn't eaten enough to move; but Gisella and Wil were also keen to get further away from the Wraithe Wolves so Seth found himself quickly out-voted[88].

The afternoon sunshine had dried their wet things and Wil was glad to wrap his cloak around his shoulders again. He tucked the hunting knife back into his boot and tied the silk first aid bag on his belt. They also had two crossbows but between them they only had four bolts; Gisella confessed that she had dropped most of her bolts when they had jumped to safety.

'Yes, but we've got Farrow!' Seth chirped. 'She's worth a hundred bolts in a fight!'

'I know,' said Wil quietly. A shadow of sorrow crossed over Mortimer's face.

'So, where do you think we should be heading, Mortimer,' Gisella asked quickly.

Mortimer looked up to the ledge where they had jumped.

'I don't think we should be trying to get back up to Skelmer Hollow – even if Tarek's body is still up there,' he said bitterly. 'Well, we've survived so far so let's follow the river down stream and get as far away from Tel Harion as we can before we go back up onto the Fells.'

It was dark before they found a suitable place to spend the night – a grassy glade with fast flowing rapids on one side and a sheer cliff that seemed to go up forever on the other. A canopy of thick trees provided shelter from any eagards that might be tempted to try to attack in the darkness.

Everyone seemed happy with the site, so Seth, Farrow and Gisella set off to catch supper while Wil and Mortimer gathered wood for another fire.

Before long Wil was skinning, plucking and gutting grouse and rabbit, while Mortimer sharpened three stakes ready to cook the meat over the fire.

'I don't know if I like grouse,' said Seth, wrinkling his nose.

'If you're hungry enough, you will,' said Mortimer. 'But if you really don't like it – well, there's all the more for us then!'

Some time later bones, stripped-clean of meat, lay discarded in and around the fire.

'Gosh, Mortimer, where did you learn to cook like that?' asked Gisella, gnawing on one last bone.

'My mother,' said Mortimer. He was lying on his side, propped up on one elbow watching the fire. 'She's convinced I'll starve out here on a Moon Chase!'

'My mother'd never let me cook!' said Seth. 'I might burn myself, or not cook something properly and get ill.'

No one commented and for a long time all four said nothing at all.

After a while Mortimer spoke quietly in the darkness.

'So, how did you find us, Seth? How did you know we were in Skelmer Hollow?'

'The map – there was a map in the dirt,' answered Seth. He threw his last bone towards the fire. It missed.

'I found the camp. You'd all gone but then I saw the map. I knew it was Skelmer because Dead Man's Beck was marked with the shape of a skull – pretty cool, I thought!'

Gisella looked at Wil, but neither said anything.

'So, if we'd only just left, why did it take you so long to find us?' asked Mortimer.

'Er... well, I'd left Saran in a hurry and forgot to bring any bolts. I had a hunt around to see if any of you lot had left any, and then I... er... I fell off Roani and broke my crossbow... *actually* I really hurt myself – look!'

Seth got to his knees and pulled up his shirt. He did indeed have a nasty black bruise over his ribs.

'How did you fall off your horse?' Gisella asked Seth. Wil could see she was trying not to laugh. 'You're training to be a chaser – being able to stay *on* a horse is a fairly important part of that job!'

'Well, yes,' said Seth. He threw a glance towards Mortimer for support, but got none. 'But Roani jumped over a stream that I didn't see because I nearly dropped my bow.'

'But I thought chasers didn't carry crossbows – I thought they were the ones with the spears and the Fellhounds?' said Wil – he was enjoying watching Seth squirm.

'Well... yes, I know. But I'm quite good with a crossbow so I thought I'd bring it instead.'

'It's just a shame you didn't remember your brain at the same time,' said Mortimer. He wasn't smiling. 'If you had, Tarek might still be alive!'

The fire crackled and popped in the silence that followed. Mortimer picked up bits of twig and threw them at the flames. Wil patted Farrow's shoulder as she lay by the fire like some huge rug. It was quite a while before Seth risked speaking again.

'I am truly sorry about Tarek, Mortimer. I just had to come. My father so desperately wants me to be a great chaser like you and what with everyone being so convinced that Wil was guilty… I just thought I could make my mark – you know, help to prove everyone right and prove to my father that I can really do it.'

Mortimer got to his feet.

'And what about you, Seth? What did you want to prove to yourself?'

He didn't wait for the boy to answer – he just turned and walked away into the darkness.

The party slept until long past dawn. When Wil opened his eyes he could see Farrow under the trees in the distance. She was tucking into[89] something. Seth was watching her eat.

Wil lay huddled in Old Barrowman's cloak. His shoulder tingled; it wasn't unpleasant at all but it reminded him that they were going back to Saran to face the Order. He was sure that Gisella would try to persuade her mother that he was innocent, but with Giles gone, Oswald Beck and Godwyn Savidge would be much harder to win round. He lay there worrying while Gisella and Mortimer argued about the route home.

'No, if we go that way we'll have to cross Hurst Fell and get down Nell's Drop *and* Esk Falls – that's one heck of a climb, Giz. How would Farrow get down?' Mortimer was saying. He had drawn another map on the ground and was using the point of a bolt to mark his preferred path.

'Well, we could head inland along the edge of Hurst and then onto Rockmoor Downs,' said Gisella.

'But we'd either have to get across the lake or go right around and up through Delve Hollow. It would take us a week to get home!' Mortimer looked at the map. 'Let's face it, Gisella; we're on the wrong side of the river.'

'You're right,' said Gisella, looking at the tumbling rapids in front of them. 'I think we're going to have to go back upstream and find a safe place to get across. At least we'll be on the right side of the Fells from there.'

CHAPTER EIGHTEEN

Ambush

Heading back the way they had walked only the night before was disappointing for everyone, but it was even worse for Wil because Mortimer and Gisella had chosen the quickest way home. Every time Wil thought about the Order his shoulder tingled; he wondered if Gisella's thigh was doing the same, or was it just a reminder that he might soon be hung as a murderer? The thought of removing the bandage filled him with dread – the label on the powder had said two days but Wil knew that two weeks wouldn't be long enough!

He trudged[90] along while the others joked and laughed; he didn't even smile when Seth slipped off the bank and fell in the river – twice!

Eventually they came to a line of huge boulders lying across the river from one bank to the other. They were green and looked very slippery but the gentle flow of the river had worn each one flat; they were perfect stepping stones.

'Right,' said Mortimer. 'I'll go first. Gisella, you're the strongest swimmer so can you go last in case someone falls in? Seth, bring Farrow and come after me. Okay? Wil, follow Seth.' He gave them a confident wink and set off, jumping from rock to rock. 'It's okay as long as you keep going,' he called when he was about halfway.

In no time at all Mortimer jumped onto the opposite bank.

'Right, Seth. Come on, but be careful. Don't stop once you've started. Farrow can swim across, don't worry about her.'

'If he makes it across I'll eat my crossbow,' Gisella whispered to Wil as Seth nearly fell off the very first stone.

But Seth jumped on to the second and third rocks with no problem at all.

'Hmm, I think you might be eating that bow, Miss Fairfax?' Wil grinned.

Farrow barked encouragement and swam around the rocks. Seth swung his leg back for his final jump and a huge salmon leapt out of the water right in front of him.

There were two splashes: one was the salmon landing back into the river – the other was Seth.

Gisella was across the rocks in a flash but Wil could see Mortimer laughing and pointing downstream. Farrow appeared from between two rocks with Seth held firmly in her teeth by the seat of his breeches. When she got to the bank she dropped him and wandered off, shaking herself from the tip of her nose to the end of her tail.

By now Gisella was laughing so much she nearly fell off the same rock! Even Wil managed a smile. Seth headed back along the bank. He was dripping wet but his smile was getting broader with every step he took.

By mid-afternoon they were heading back down the river on the right side. When they got to Thesker Pyke the high river cliffs flattened into the grey, scrubby grass and grey sky of the fells; in the distance Wil could hear a roaring waterfall.

'Welcome to Nell's Reach, Wil,' said Mortimer. He nodded towards the sound of the waterfall. 'Down there is Nell's Drop and Esk Falls. Goatmed Scarp's further along, too. It's all just one very big drop.'

Wil decided not to have a look.

'Well, I reckon we're about three hours walk from Saran,' said Mortimer. He was carrying the carcass of the deer that Farrow had caught earlier across his shoulders. 'There's still plenty of light left so let's get on home and I'll cook a celebration feast when we get there.'

They marched along the top of Nell's Reach, laughing and joking – everyone except Wil, that is. But no one seemed to notice that he wasn't joining in. Below, the river was flowing faster now on its way downstream. Up ahead, Wil could see a narrow valley, filled with pine, oak and beech trees.

'Great, Hester Beck!' said Mortimer, pointing to a little stream that ran through the valley before joining the river on it's way to Esk Falls. 'I love this place. I used to come up here when I was a kid with my father and uncle. It's great for trout!'

'D'you ever think of anything other than your stomach, Mortimer Merridown?' Gisella grinned.

'Hey, look,' said Mortimer. 'There's so much great stuff to eat out here. It's a crime not to try it!'

Seth pulled a face. 'I don't know if I'd like trout. My mother says they've got too many bones and I might choke.'

'And *Mortimer* says, I think you ought to stop listening to your mother, Seth Tanner!' said Mortimer.

Gisella and Wil laughed.

'Come on,' said Mortimer. 'Let's see if we can catch a nice big trout. We haven't had any lunch yet and I'm *starving!*'

Mortimer was right – Seth was forced to agree that the fish was absolutely delicious; there was even enough for Farrow, which she gulped down in two grateful mouthfuls.

Wil watched the others enviously; now that they were nearing their home Gisella, Mortimer and Seth were enjoying themselves. After all, Wil thought, they were going home; he was going to face being hung! His shoulder tingled again.

A man's voice suddenly came from behind them.

"Well, well – what do we have here? How lovely – a picnic! Can we *all* join in?'

Wil swallowed his last mouthful of salmon. He knew that voice. He turned. A tall, thin man with a straggly black beard was standing at the top of the hill.

'Sir Jerad Tinniswood,' thought Wil. 'This is not going to be good!'

Tinniswood's sunken eyes were blood-shot and he looked as if he hadn't had a proper night's sleep or a good meal for a very long time. Around him were gathered a group of thuggish-looking[91] men on sweating horses; each one had either a crossbow or a sling shot – all of which were, at that moment, aimed at the picnicking group.

Farrow shifted her weight back onto her haunches and prepared to spring – Sir Jerad guessed her plan.

'If I were you I would keep that mutt under control. She might be fairly effective against four, but *fifteen*, all with bows aimed at her heart – I think this time she might lose!' sneered Tinniswood. A few of the men nearest him nodded – one spat on the ground.

'What do you want?' demanded Mortimer, slowly wiping his fishy hands in his trousers.

'My dear boy – it's not really what *I* want that counts. You see, my new friends here were simply going about their business the other day – *venison rustling*[92], you know – when four of their colleagues were set upon by an animal that, they tell me, looked *amazingly* like this one.' Tinniswood gestured towards Farrow, pretending to be shocked. 'And now, strangely enough – they want revenge!'

'No! It couldn't have been – we were – no, not Farrow!' Seth looked in confusion from the smirking Tinniswood to Wil and back again.

'Yes – *Farrow!*' spat Tinniswood. 'It's lucky, boy, that the *whole* of Saran chose to blame young Master Calloway here. The trial sounded great fun! And watching you disappearing into the dusk,' he said addressing Wil directly. 'Clinging on to that poor girl for dear life – she looked *most* unhappy – good-looking boy like you, too. Hilarious!'

'How d'you know about that?' demanded Wil.

'Oh, I have my sources.' His eyes flashed towards Gisella.

'What do you mean?' exclaimed Gisella. 'I haven't told anyone anything!'

'Not you, young lady. Ha, ha!'

Gisella looked confused, then she whispered, 'Mother?'

'What a bright girl you are after all, Miss Fairfax! I must mention it to Fermina next time I see her –

you're *such* a disappointment to her. Did you know that?'

Gisella looked shocked. Wil remembered how Tinniswood had tried to turn him against Lady Élanor in the jail and could feel anger rising with every word this malicious man said.

'Don't listen to him, Gisella – everything he says is pure poison!'

Tinniswood ignored Wil.

'Well, this really is the most *amazing* luck! A precious son, a loving daughter, a chef *and* a seer!'

'What are you going to do with us?' demanded Wil.

'Well, first I'm going to insist that your chef here cooks that deer, and it had better be delicious,' he answered in a slow drawl.

'I will not!' said Mortimer.

'Oh, you will, boy – because if you don't,' Tinniswood calmly took a bow from his nearest henchman, clicked it into position and pointed it at Gisella. 'I'll put an arrow through Miss Fairfax's pretty thigh… and if you serve it up burnt, I'll put an arrow in the other one!' The men around him laughed.

'How do I know that you won't just wait until I've cooked it and then shoot us anyway?' said Mortimer.

'You don't,' answered Tinniswood. 'Now get on with it, I'm hungry!'

Mortimer started to prepare the deer for cooking while Sir Jerad ordered his men to tie up the others.

'When do we get the hound?' growled one of the thugs. He pulled the rope tight around Wil's legs and the hilt of the hunting knife dug into Wil's ankle – he tried not to flinch and prayed that the man wouldn't notice the weapon. He didn't.

'We'll need her when we go over Tel Harion. You can do what you like with her once we get back to Armelia. But remember, *the seer is mine!*' Tinniswood answered.

'Why are you taking us there?' Gisella asked.

'Because, my pretty girl, you will be useful – *of course!*'

He spoke very close to Gisella's face and then kissed her on the cheek. Gisella jerked away. Wil wished he could reach his knife.

'You keep away from her, Tinniswood, or I'll–'

'You'll *what* exactly, young Calloway? W*hat exactly do you think you will accomplish trussed up like a chicken?*'

He strode towards Wil, grinning. Suddenly Tinniswood spotted Wil's belt.

'What have you got there, boy – in that pink purse? I bet its gold; silly to wear it where *anyone* can see it!'

'It's not gold – it's nothing.' Wil tried to move away but Tinniswood snatched at the bag – the cord that kept it fastened to his belt snapped.

'Let me see, what do we have here?'

'That's mine, give it back!' shouted Wil.

Tinniswood plunged his skinny hand into the silk bag and pulled out a smaller plain cloth package. He held it up. Wil could see a familiar label and hoped that Tally hadn't put Belladonna or Hemlock into the bag – *just in case!*

Tinniswood held the handwritten label at arm's length and squinted at it.

'What is this?'

He read out loud.

'*Juniper… excellent accompaniment to venison. Crush and rub into meat before cooking. For best results cook over an open fire. Best before–* Is this a joke, boy?'

Wil swallowed a smile and hoped his relief didn't show.

'Mortimer gave it to me… to look after when he went up for the chase,' he said and caught Mortimer's eye. Mortimer blinked and then said quickly:

'Oh, yer… Thanks, Wil – I was just about to ask for it actually – juniper – hmm, good idea!' But he didn't sound very convincing.

'Is this a trick?' Tinniswood demanded. He plunged his hand into the bag again and pulled out another plain cloth bag. Once again he read the label dangling from it.

'*Garlic – delicious with all meats. Not advisable for game.*

Rub into meat and leave to rest for three hours. Ideal for casseroles and roasts. Best before the next full moons.'

Mortimer and Wil exchanged amused glances. Mortimer spoke again.

'*Oh, absolutely!* Garlic with venison – ooh, never a good idea, unless you've got lots of time for the flavour to really go into the meat. My mother always says –'

'I don't care what your mother, father or Aunty Nelly says about cooking with damned garlic! Just cook our supper... and if it isn't absolutely delicious, I'll shoot Master Tanner, too. It's his hound I'm after anyway!'

Tinniswood chucked the bag at Mortimer and marched off to the river where he stooped to throw a handful of water over his face.

Mortimer grinned.

'Don't worry, Wil. I don't know what this bag is but I'll keep it safe for you – if I give it back now, Prince Charming over there will suspect something!' he whispered and tucked the little bag into his own belt.

As the delicious aroma of cooking meat wafted tantalisingly[93] around the little valley Tinniswood gave the order for Mortimer to be tied up with the others. No one spoke while they ate; conversation was replaced by the sound of chomping[94] and burping. By the time they had finished it was almost dark.

Grease glistened off Tinniswood's beard. He wiped

his sleeve hard across his mouth and burped loudly before he spoke.

'Right, we'll camp here tonight and start out at first light tomorrow. I want to be across Tel Harion by late afternoon.'

'When do we get the hound?' asked a mean-looking man leaning against a tree picking his teeth with the point of a dagger.

'Yeah, and the girl... we want the girl, too!' growled another. The others muttered in agreement.

'Gentlemen,' soothed[95] Tinniswood with his palms up as he spoke, 'Once we're over Tel Harion and away from any risk of Wraithe Wolf attacks, you can have the hound *and* the girl – but until then, they are *my* prisoners. Is that understood?'

Wil went cold at these words. They had to get away. He just didn't know how!

CHAPTER NINETEEN

Escape into the Night

Wil woke in pitch blackness; it was so dark that he couldn't tell if his eyes were open or still closed. A thick fog covered the valley like a blanket and smothered any moonlight shining elsewhere on the Fells.

At first he couldn't work out exactly what had woken him up. Was it the loud snoring of the guard? Or the cold night air chilling his nose and ears? But then there was a soft tap on his boot. He jerked his foot away thinking that it might be a rat hoping to get a nibble on the deer carcass.

Tap, tap, tap.

There it was again – very gentle, but definitely there. He jerked his foot again and shut his eyes tight, although there wasn't any point – he couldn't see a thing anyway! There was silence for a few moments, but it was the kind of silence that told Wil that there was something there.

He listened.

Suddenly there was a brisk flutter of wings – a definitely rather cross flutter, and something was dropped onto the ground right by his face. Then he felt a very soft tap on his nose and a low, 'Crronk!'

> *Juniper...*
> *excellent accompaniment to venison.*
> *Crush and rub into meat before cooking.*
> *For best results cook over an open fire.*
> *Best before: The last full moons of the first equinox*

Wil opened his eyes. Pricilla's beak was almost touching his nose, and in it was one of the small, plain packages from the pink silk bag. She kept picking it up and dropping it; then she picked up the label. To Wil's amazement the writing was glowing silver.

'Yes, I know about that, Pricilla. Unfortunately I don't think its going to help right now!' Wil whispered. She flicked the label over and held it up again. More elegant silver writing shone from the reverse side[96]:

> *Juniper...*
> *excellent sleeping drug if you are being held captive by greedy thieves who don't share their supper!*
> *Effective for 6-8 hours.*
> *Best before: Use Now!*

Wil read the label three times then he wriggled over to the nearest sleeping guard and nudged him with his foot.

The guard snored loudly. Wil kicked him. The man turned over and cuddled up to the man sleeping next to him. One final, very hard boot in the man's shin – this man was defiantly not going to wake up anytime soon.

By now, Wil's hands were numb from the tight bindings. He tried to loosen the ropes to get free, but it was no use. He rolled onto his side.

'Pricilla, undo the knot.'

She didn't move.

'Pricilla, behind me, my hands are tied – *undo the knot!*' he hissed again.

She still didn't move. It was hopeless; Pricilla just didn't seem to understand. He took a deep breath and tried once more.

'Look Pricilla, I can't help the others unless my hands are untied, so *pleeese*, will you help me?'

'Crronk!'

The raven jumped onto his bottom and onto the ground behind him, then, at last Wil felt her tug at the bindings.

'Oh, well,' he thought to himself; 'My mother did always tell me that *"please"* would get me a long way!'

Wil felt the rope go loose.

'Thank you, Pricilla!' He pulled his hands free and rubbed his sore wrists. Pricilla nodded her silky black head at him and took off into the night sky.

The label lay on the ground. Wil read it again and wondered how long it was since Tinniswood and his men had eaten. It had certainly been dark but Wil had no idea how long they had been asleep.

He pushed the label into his pocket and shook Mortimer's shoulder. Mortimer jumped the moment Wil touched him.

'What... who... what's happened?'

'It's me, Wil,' Wil whispered. 'Shhh, Mortimer. It's okay. We need to wake the others and get out of here.' He gently shook Mortimer by the shoulder. 'Listen to me, Mortimer. Did you eat any of the meat?'

Mortimer blinked and coughed loudly.

'Er, what? No... don't think so, no.'

He shook his head. He was making a lot of noise. Wil spoke quickly.

'Mort, ssh! We've got to get out of here. I don't know how much time we've got. It's the juniper – I'll explain later. I'll wake Gisella. Go and get Seth. But do it quietly!'

Mortimer's expression said it all.

'You can't wake him, can you?' said Wil.

'No. And I found this next to him!' Mortimer held up a bone – it was picked clean. 'He was right by the fire – I think he ate some of the meat.'

Wil knew it wasn't really the boy's fault, after all how could Seth have known that the meat had been drugged? But things *always* seemed to happen to Seth. Wil looked at Mortimer and Gisella and shook his head.

'How that boy ever became a Fellman is completely beyond me!'

'You're not going to be able to carry him all the way back to Saran, Mortimer! We need to hide somewhere until he wakes up,' Gisella was saying as they struggled up the side of the steep valley. Seth was flopped over Mortimer's shoulder.

'I'll be fine, Giz – honestly. I've carried injured Fellmen far heavier than Seth off the Fell after a Moon Chase. Remember when that Bearer, Erik Pederson, accidentally got shot? Shadow went lame so I had to carry Erik – he was a real lump!'

'Why can't Seth ride on Farrow?' Wil asked innocently.

Mortimer and Gisella stopped walking.

'Why do you think she could do that, Wil?' said Gisella.

'She's a hound, not a horse!' said Mortimer looking genuinely confused. Wil had another idea.

'Well, how about I go back and steal a couple of horses?'

Gisella looked horrified.

'Wil, it's too dangerous. Anyway, you can't ride!'

'And what if they wake up?' said Mortimer. But he was panting so hard that Wil knew they didn't have a choice.

'I know, but Seth must have eaten at about the same time as the others so we'll know we're in trouble when he starts to wake up,' reasoned Wil. 'And by the look of him right now, that's not going to be for ages!'

Gisella moved to Wil's side.

'Well, if you're going, Wil, I'm going, too. We'll get two horses so we can all ride home,' said Gisella in a tone that meant there was no point arguing.

Mortimer agreed but looked worried.

'Okay, but if you hear my whistle; two short bursts means Seth's waking up – which means that lot down there will be, too!'

'I wish I still had my crossbow, though,' said Gisella. 'Did you see what they did with it, Mort?'

'One of Tinniswood's thugs put it on the fire – sorry Giz.'

Gisella looked more determined than ever. 'Right, come on Wil. Let's show them that they aren't the only ones who can steal livestock!'

She set off back down the steep, grassy slope; Wil looked at Mortimer and shrugged.

'We'll be back as quickly as we can,' he said, trying to sound a lot more confident than he felt. Then he set off after Gisella.

Wil and Gisella stumbled through the bracken and emerged[97] breathless out of the fog. All around them were the sounds of regular breathing and loud snores; the horses were tied to a rope between two trees close to the river.

'I can't believe you don't know how to ride, Wil!' Gisella hissed as she untied two of the horses nearest them. By luck, no one had bothered to take off their bridles.

'It never came up at home,' Wil whispered. He looked around but there was no sign of any saddles. 'The horses at home are used in the fields – the other kids rode them at the end of the day, but... well, I just never wanted to.'

'So when was the first time you ever got on a horse?' Gisella asked as she jumped easily onto the one nearest her.

'Two days ago – when I got on Olivia's,' replied Wil.

'Well, in that case you'd better ride with me, Wil. I can't see us getting back to Mortimer otherwise – especially with no saddle!' Gisella held the reins of both horses in one hand and held her other arm out to help Wil up.

But as Wil stepped forward he spotted a broadsword resting against a tree.

'Hang on Gisella – that might come in handy.'

He clasped his hand around the hilt... and felt a strong hand grasp his ankle.

'GO GISELLA! GO!'

'Wil, what the–'

'JUST GO! GET OUT OF HERE – GO!'

'Stop right there, you little...' growled the voice belonging to the hand.

Without thinking, Wil swung the sword downwards. It sliced through the rustler's wrist like butter. His scream filled the valley. Wil didn't look down. All of a sudden there were voices everywhere.

'Go Gisella. Get out of here. Get to the others!'

He slapped Gisella's horse hard on the rump. She was still holding the reins of the second horse. Both animals galloped away into the dark.

In the next second he heard a long whistle blast. Had Gisella raised the alarm? Would she be able to stay on? Then Wil heard pounding hooves going in the direction of Mortimer, Farrow and Seth and guessed she had.

In the camp, there was chaos. The fog was lifting but it was still difficult to see more than a few feet. Men were shouting and horses were whinnying and rearing. Wil ducked down, untied the rope that held the remaining horses and waved his arms frantically. As the terrified animals fled into the milky darkness[98] Wil headed for the river; this did mean going straight towards the camp; but, he thought, it would be the last thing they'd be expecting!

CHAPTER TWENTY

Upstream or Downstream?

Wil knew he'd got to the river when he ran straight into it. He crouched in the freezing water, still clutching the stolen sword. He could hear angry shouts from the camp, including Tinniswood – he was livid.

'*FIND HIM – FIND THE SEER! I DON'T CARE ABOUT THE OTHERS – JUST FIND THAT BOY AND BRING HIM TO ME!*'

Wil lowered himself into the bitterly cold water. The sounds of shouting and splashing told Wil that there were men on both banks now – they were spreading out to search for him. He knew it wouldn't be long before they found their horses, too.

It was too risky to try to catch-up with the others but Wil's teeth were now chattering so loudly that he was in serious danger of being heard if he stayed where he was. He had no choice; the only way out was to follow the river. But which way? Upstream would take him right through the middle of the camp; downstream would lead to Esk Falls. Downstream *felt* like the better option. And once he was far enough away, he reasoned[99], he would be able to get back on dry land. So, with a quick look to make sure no-one was nearby, he stepped into the middle of the river.

Half-wading, half swimming, Wil let the flowing water carry him away. In the distance he could hear barking and angry shouting. Then he heard a sound that made his already chilled blood freeze. A girl screamed – a loud, long scream of pain, anger and fear.

'*Gisella!*'

Wil was desperate to turn back. He scrambled out of the water onto the bank, stood and listened, but Esk Falls was so loud it was drowning out everything else. It was dawn now and the fog looked pink in the early morning light. He stood at the water's edge and thought: would he be putting his friends in danger if he went back? But his question was answered almost immediately.

A figure on horseback was walking towards him out of the fog. Wil called out hopefully.

'Gisella?'

But as the figure drew closer, Wil realised he was wrong.

He jumped back into the river but it was too late.

'Master Calloway – did you *really* think you would get away that easily?'

Sir Jerad Tinniswood stopped his horse at the edge of the river. Wil ducked down and said nothing.

Tinniswood urged his horse right to the edge of the bank and leant over its neck. Wil was shaking uncontrollably with the cold.

'You left a trail!' He smirked and flicked something into the water in front of Wil; as it floated downstream Wil could see that it was the juniper label. 'I heard what Élanor said to you, boy. You can see into the minds of others. You would not believe how long I've been out here trying to find out that bitch's great secret – the whereabouts of her legacy. You are going to help me to find it. Then I'm going to take you and the legacy back to Lord Rexmoore. For too long I have been a servant to that man and his grasping wife! Finally I will be rewarded for my loyalty!'

Tinniswood ranted on about hard work and devotion, but Wil was now chilled to the core. He began to feel strangely warm – all he wanted to do was go to sleep. His concentration drifted and the sword slipped from his numb fingers.

To his amazement, Lady Élanor walked out of the fog and stopped right behind Tinniswood's horse. *'Open your mind Wil – the horse – use the horse.'* Then she was gone.

Wil blinked. Tinniswood was still following him. He was talking as if he hadn't seen anything unusual.

'Look, boy. You might as well give up and get out of the water. Or shall I just wait until the cold gets the better of you?'

'And what if I refuse to help you?' shivered Wil.

'Well, I'll just give you back to my new friends. They are very keen to see you again; one is especially keen since you cut off his hand! I can't remember exactly what he said he would do if he found you but it didn't sound *particularly* friendly!'

Tinniswood carried on talking but Wil's chilled brain was unable to listen. He heard Lady Élanor's voice again. She whispered, '*Open your mind Wil. The horse – use the horse.*'

He closed his eyes and felt the water flow around him. He imagined Tinniswood's horse standing on the bank of the river. He imagined the horse rearing and bucking. He pictured the scene over and ove... Nothing happened. He tried again, but he was starting to lose consciousness... Still nothing.

With every bit of strength he had left he imagined the horse rearing up and stamping on Tinniswood after he crashed to the ground... Then Wil saw another shape coming slowly out of the fog. Its long black body scraped along the ground as it crept towards its prey. Wil kept his eyes firmly shut. He could hear it snarling, could smell rotting meat and damp, filthy hair. He pictured a pair of massive fangs dripping with blood, and long barbed claws ...

There was an enormous splash. Wil opened his eyes.

The horse was galloping away into the fog – Tinniswood was no longer on its back, he was in the water! The huge Wraithe Wolf was nowhere to be seen.

Suddenly Wil had the advantage. He tried to scramble up the bank but a strong hand clutched at his boot. It threw him off balance and he toppled back into the water – right on top of Tinniswood.

The current was dragging them faster now. Wil's leg bashed hard against a sharp rock. He cried out in frustration and pain. The river wasn't very deep but he couldn't stand, luckily Tinniswood seemed to be having the same problem.

Tinniswood grabbed Wil's ankle and pulled him underwater. He wished he hadn't let go of the sword and kicked out – hard. Tinniswood gasped and breathed in a huge lungful of water – Wil had caught him right between the legs. He kicked away as hard as he could and crawled up onto a flat rock. The water was bubbling all around him. The sound of Esk Falls was deafening now. There just didn't seem to be a way out of the river.

'Ha, ha! You are beaten, Calloway,' shouted Tinniswood. He was clinging to a rock closer to the bank. 'Look, give yourself up, boy. The only way out is past me. I'll see you on the bank!'

Wil had no intention of giving up. He looked along the opposite bank: the water there was flowing exceptionally fast. Jagged rocks jutted out of deep pools.

There would be no escape that way and Wil was much too tired to try going back upstream.

He tucked his knees under his chin and wrapped his arms around his legs. He could hear Tinniswood laughing. But then Wil felt the hunting knife; it was still tucked in the lining of his boot!

He looked over the rapids again. White foam and spray swirled around the rocks. Other streams joined the river a little way down adding to the amount and speed of the water. But on the opposite bank, just before the first of these streams, was a huge weeping willow. Its arching branches trailed into the surging torrent[100] like long tentacles. If he could reach that tree he could catch hold of the branches and climb out before he got swept down to Esk Falls.

'So boy,' shouted Tinniswood. 'What's it to be? Shall I wait until you pass out or are you going to be sensible and come to me?'

'Na! Think I'll pass[101],' said Wil and rolled off the rock.

The current was much stronger than Wil had expected and he was bounced from rock to rock as the water swept him along. He could see the branches getting nearer. All he had to do was reach out and.... Wil came to an abrupt halt. His foot had jammed between two rocks; it was stuck fast.

A shout from behind him made Wil look round.

Tinniswood was coming towards him. Wil struggled. The hunting knife was stopping his leg from coming free. Tinniswood was nearly on him.

With a deep breath Wil ducked under the water, grabbed the knife and pulled as hard as he could. Just as his leg came free Tinniswood grabbed his cloak.

Wil was now very close to the willow. He stretched out one arm and fought Tinniswood off with the other. Another second…

Wil grabbed a handful of slender tentacles, swung around and, with a yell, stabbed wildly at the water.

All of a sudden Tinniswood let go. The water all around Wil turned dark, dark red. He kicked Tinniswood back out into the river and clung to the willow branches. As Tinniswood disappeared into the rapids all Wil could see was the man's outstretched hand then… he was gone.

CHAPTER TWENTY-ONE

Rescue

The fog had gone and the pink and orange rays of dawn lit up Goatmed Scarp way off in the distance. Far too exhausted to try to climb the steep river bank, Wil lay at the water's edge.

He remembered the terrible scream he'd heard just before Tinniswood had found him; it was definitely a girl's scream. At least Mortimer still had the enchanted first aid bag so if Gisella was injured – maybe it would help to save her? Then Wil thought about the juniper and Seth. He knew Seth couldn't have known the meat had been drugged but it was difficult not to be angry with him. If the boy hadn't eaten the meat they would have been able to wake him up, and they wouldn't have gone back to steal the horses; and no one would have woken up; and they would probably by now have been back in Saran... and Gisella wouldn't have screamed...

He heard a sound... more horses hooves. He crawled up the bank and peered onto the fell, dreading what he might see. Tinniswood's horse was plodding towards him complete with bridle... and saddle!

It took Wil three attempts before he managed to get onto the horse facing the right way. Feeling very pleased with himself, he held the reins in his fist and looked straight between the horse's ears.

The horse snorted.

'Okay, so how do you make these things go?' Wil muttered to himself. He was also trying not to look down – it was much higher than it looked!

He shuffled his bottom back and forward in the saddle but the horse didn't move.

Then he shouted '*YAR!*' It didn't work.

He flicked the reins – the horse plunged its head forward to nibble on the grass and pulled Wil straight out of the saddle and over its neck. The horse stopped eating and sniffed him.

Wil lay on his back looking up at the animal. 'Okay,' he thought, 'I don't really want to go back to Saran anyway and I'm sure Gisella and the others'll be fine. So why don't I just give up, let this nag go and walk home to Mistlegard?'

'*Because,*' said a voice in his head, '*you don't know if Gisella, Seth, Mortimer and Farrow are alright and if you don't go back, you'll be looking over your shoulder forever in case the Order are behind you. Go back and sort this out!*'

As he lay looking up into the brightening sky, arguing with his conscience, a tiny black dot moved

across the sky towards him, getting larger as it got nearer. Wil smiled.

'The thing is, Pricilla; I can't get it moving. I managed to get on but it wouldn't go and I fell off again. *Please* can you help me? I've got to find the others – I think they're in trouble!' Wil said to the raven as politely as he could – he was getting more worried by the minute.

Pricilla cocked her head to one side. Then she fluttered over to the horse and landed between its ears. The horse made no effort to get the bird to move.

'Prruk, Prruk!' chattered Pricilla. Wil watched.

The horse walked back to Wil and lowered itself right down onto the ground. Then it looked at him and snorted.

'Am I supposed to get on now?' he asked looking at Pricilla.

'Crronk!'

'Just checking.' He stepped across the horse and lowered his backside gingerly onto the saddle.

The horse then slowly got up – front feet first. Wil closed his eyes and clung on. Pricilla flew high into the air, swirled round in an arc and returned, fluttering her broad black wings right in front of the horse. The animal set off at a walk. Wil tried to remember how Olivia had held the reins when he had ridden behind her and did his best to stay in the saddle.

Although progress was slow, Wil at least felt that it *was* progress; Pricilla swooped[102] down when they needed to change direction, and by mid morning Wil was starting to feel quite pleased with himself – it was now several hours since he had last fallen off!

Wil was starving. There was a bag buckled to the front of the saddle and, trying not to look down, he found some slices of stale bread and a piece of meat. He decided not to try the meat in case it was the drugged venison, but he devoured almost all of the bread in an instant; although he kept a small piece for Pricilla, which she took from his outstretched hand. Once she had eaten she disappeared for quite a while.

Wil felt very nervous riding alone across the open Fell and was glad when they reached a sheltered gully.

'Crronk, Crronk!' Pricilla landed on a rocky ledge right in front of them.

The horse stopped.

The raven looked at Wil with her beady eyes and cocked her head to one side in what was becoming a very familiar look.

'I suppose you want me to get off?' he said.

'Crronk!' she answered, flexing her wings.

Wil slowly dragged his leg over the back of the saddle and slid awkwardly to the ground; his legs were numb and as he landed a pain shot up his back.

Pricilla was staring towards a clump of pine trees some way off. Wil was squinting in the same direction, trying to see what she was looking at when a gentle breeze filled Wil's nose with the most delicious smell of cooking.

'*Mortimer!*' Wil whispered. But why hadn't Pricilla just taken him straight there? He turned to ask her but she'd gone again.

Just a little annoyed, Wil tied the horse to a scrubby bush and politely asked it to wait there. '*Well, it worked with Pricilla,*' he thought. The horse did indeed stand still.

High in the sky the two moons were already shining down – it would be night again very soon. There was still no sign of Pricilla so Wil decided to wait until it got dark before going to get a closer look. He sat down, rolled his cloak into a pillow and tried to get comfortable while he waited; within minutes he was asleep.

This time Wil was woken up by heavy breathing. He squinted into the fading light. The hot breath on his neck was coming from the horse.

'Are you trying to tell me something – or just being annoying?' asked Wil. He got to his feet and looked across towards the distant camp. To his horror, he could see that whoever was over there was preparing to leave!

He told the horse to stay and pulled the hood of his cloak over his head; then he climbed out of the gully.

The fell was eerily quiet. Wil tried his best to work out who was there, or what was going on... Then he saw them – *in his mind.* He could see Gisella; she had a nasty cut on her head; Seth was bound and gagged. Then he saw Mortimer, who was tucking Wil's pink silk purse back into his belt. There were also three men. One walked up to Gisella and stroked her cheek. She pulled away. Wil could hear their cruel laughter. All he wanted to do was march over and kill the men there and then. Farrow was at the edge of the camp; she was tied to a tree with a short chain. There were also three horses tethered not far away; all were saddled-up and packed. Mortimer was talking.

'But we can't go onto Tel Harion with only one hound – we'd be dead before we got up onto the first slopes!'

'Look, boy – we've been babysitting too long already. We're takin' you[103] to Lord Rexmoore tonight and that's the end of it! And you'd better pray that Tinniswood was right about how valuable you are!'

Wil scrambled back down to the horse. Pricilla was already there. A thought struck him.

'It was you, Pricilla – wasn't it? *You* showed me what happened to Seth up on the Fell and you did it again just now!'

The raven spread her wings and twitched her head to one side – Wil was right, he knew it!

There was only one way to rescue the others; Wil had to make Farrow understand that he needed her help... then another thought struck him.

'Pricilla – I need one more favour... please.'

The raven cocked her head.

'I promise this isn't *too* dangerous!' he said quickly. 'Pricilla, will you bring Tinniswood's horse down to the other side of the trees and wait for me – please? I need to undo that chain; I'm going to get Farrow to attack those men so that I can untie Gisella, Mortimer and Seth. They can take the horses and get back to Saran.'

The look on the raven's face told Wil that if she could have spoken she would have said, 'Are you completely mad? You can't even communicate with your horse!'

But she couldn't speak – luckily.

Wil checked his hunting knife was safe in his boot, pulled his hood low over his head and made his way back up onto the fell.

It was pitch dark now and halfway between the gully and the copse he fell into a rabbit-hole; then he cracked his knee on a raised tree root and bit his lip.

When he reached the copse Wil couldn't see Gisella, Mortimer, Seth or Farrow anywhere. The men were checking the horses. Wil could hear them talking

'So what do you think he'll do with 'em?'

'Don't know, don't care. As long as 'e pays us for delivering 'em!'

'I reckon 'e'll 'old 'em to ransom – the girl's gotta be worth a bit – pretty thing like that'.

'I 'ope so – that mutt's gotta be worth a bit, too! Maybe it was worth losing Duncan and the others after all!'

'*And* – don't forget – we've still got the deer in Thesker Pyke!'

They all laughed.

Wil crept around to the other side of the copse. The bright full-moons of the Moon Chase were now two thin silver crescents[104] that provided very little light to guide his way. He walked into an unseen branch and swore; so he ducked down to avoid doing the same thing at the next tree and nearly fell over Farrow.

She sat up, suddenly alert. Wil crouched low in the pitch-darkness, closed his eyes and concentrated on the Fellhound.

His heart felt like it was going to pound out of his chest. Very slowly he could feel a second set of beats. But this heart-beat was slower and deeper than his – as if it was beating in a larger chest. It felt very odd and made him feel slightly sick. He opened his eyes. Farrow was staring at him.

'Farrow, wait.' Wil let the words flow around his mind – hoping that Farrow would pick up his thoughts and understand. She stayed absolutely still.

Wil tried to keep his mind on Farrow while he took a step closer; he tripped over yet another tree root. His concentration broke. Fallow jumped to her feet.

'*DROP!*'

With his lips pressed firmly together he'd somehow managed to stop the word from bursting out of his mouth. To his amazement, Farrow dropped flat to the ground.

'What was that?' said one of the men.

'What was what? Didn't 'ear nothing!' said another.

'Over by the 'ound. She just did something!'

'I reckon you ate too much of that rabbit, 'arry – given yourself indigestion! Come on let's get this lot movin' or we'll be 'ere all night – *again!*'

Wil stayed stretched-out on the damp ground. Farrow started to pant. Wil could feel her excitement. He carefully pulled the iron pin that fixed her collar to the chain.

'*Wait, Farrow,*' he thought.

She lay still but Wil could feel that she was ready to explode into life.

Wil could see the orange glow of the dying fire through the dark trees. Then, at last, he saw Gisella – she was staring at the men with deep loathing. Mortimer was sitting next to her. Their hands were tied tight behind their backs. There was no sign of Seth.

One of the men grabbed Gisella by the arm and lifted her to her feet. She cried out. Wil gripped the metal pin so tightly it cut into his hand. He gave the word:

'*GO FARROW – GET THEM!*'

Farrow charged at the man holding Gisella. They both screamed but Farrow hit her target and went in search of the others. She left Gisella, still screaming.

'Gisella, Gisella – it's me. It's Wil!' He grabbed her shoulders and held her until she stopped screaming.

'Wil – where on earth… How? We thought you were dead!' She burst into tears and flung her arms around his neck.

'It's good to see you, too, Giz, but this really isn't the time.' Wil ran to untie Mortimer. His face was filthy and he had a black eye.

Another blood-curdling scream suggested that Farrow was taking care of things elsewhere.

'Where's Seth?' Wil asked, looking around.

'We're over here – I can't untie him!' called Gisella. Her desperate voice was almost drowned out by the sound of Farrow barking and snarling – and men shrieking.

Wil and Mortimer ran to help.

'Blimey, how many ropes did they use, Seth?' asked Wil.

'He made a run for it this morning!' said Mortimer.

'Yes, and I really thought I'd get away, too. But that blinking horse fell down a fox hole. I think I've broken my leg!'

Wil glanced at Mortimer – neither of them said a word.

'Stop right there!' said a gruff voice behind them. Wil and Mortimer froze. 'Call off your dog – or I'll shoot.'

Farrow leapt into the clearing. Wil, Mortimer and Seth all spoke at once.

'Wait!' Farrow stopped.

'Right; nice and slow – seein' as I'm the only one who's armed.' He pointed his crossbow at Gisella as he spoke. 'You, girl. Tie your mate back up – and your *new* friend!'

Then he took a second look at Wil.

'You're that seer Tinniswood was so interested in! 'e went after you. What 'appened to 'im?'

'Last I saw he was taking a swim off Esk Falls,' said Wil.

'You little… Hey, I thought I said tie your mate up, girl!' The lone rustler swung his bow back towards Gisella, who ducked. Wil heard something whistle past his ear and the man dropped to the ground – stone dead.

Wil and Mortimer turned. There sat Seth looking

very pleased with himself.

'Funny what people leave lying around, isn't it?' he said with a grin. He was holding a crossbow – his feet were still tightly bound.

'I thought Gisella said that she couldn't untie you?' Mortimer said, looking from Seth to Gisella and back again.

'Well, the legs seem to be a bit of a problem, but she managed to loosen my arms. I just pulled my hands through – I think I've got a bit of rope-burn though!'

'And where did you learn to shoot like that, Seth?' asked Wil.

Seth's eyes twinkled.

'Oh, Cae and I practice all the time at home. To be honest, I prefer the crossbow – but don't tell Farrow – or my father!'

CHAPTER TWENTY-TWO

Wil's Choice

By the time they had hidden the bodies in the copse, Wil had made up his mind.

Mortimer, Gisella and Seth took a horse each.

'Come on, Wil, you'd better ride with me,' said Mortimer offering his hand down to Wil.

'Er, no thanks, Mort. Tinniswood's horse got me this far and, if my plan works out, it'll be right on the other side of these trees.'

'What? You rode here – *on your own!*' exclaimed Gisella. She looked genuinely impressed.

'Yep – well, I sat on; the horse did the rest. I had a bit of help with steering, too... but hey, I got here, didn't I?'

'Okay, we'll come with you. We can all ride back together. Even in the dark, I'm pretty sure I can remember the way,' said Mortimer grinning. Wil could hear the excitement in his friend's voice; it was obvious that he, Gisella and Seth were desperate to get back home.

'No, er... it's OK. You go on and I'll catch you up!'

'You're not going to come with us – are you, Wil?' said Gisella, but Wil could tell that she already knew the answer.

'Yer, course I am! I'm just going to get the horse – I'll follow you,' he lied, turning away as he spoke.

'Wil, think about it, mate. If you don't face the Order now, you'll never be able to come to Saran again, and if they catch you...' Mortimer didn't finish. Wil answered without turning around.

'I just can't. You know what happened to my shoulder. Godwyn Savidge said, 'killed *or* injured'. They'll hang me whatever you lot tell them!'

Seth looked like he'd been struck by something hard.

'You got injured!' he exclaimed. 'When was that?'

'Not that it matters now, but it was on the Moon Chase – when Leon got knocked out. Becky was there – she's probably told everyone by now.' Wil didn't try to hide the bitterness in his voice. 'They'll blame me for Giles, too, I know it. Sorry Gisella, but your mother was as convinced as Savidge and Beck. They'll hang me, Giz.'

A single tear trickled down Gisella's face, but she didn't say anything.

'I'm so sorry, Wil,' said Seth. 'I'd fight your corner[105], if you came with us.'

'And Gisella and I'll tell them that without you we wouldn't have survived the Moon Chase – or the journey home! Please come with us, Wil,' begged Mortimer. But Wil's mind was made up.

'I can't – I'm sorry. I need to go home – to *my* home. But… thanks anyway.'

Gisella nodded. Her eyes sparkled with unspent tears.

Farrow was sitting close by. Wil walked up and scratched the hound's ear. She leant into his hand and groaned in appreciation.

'Keep looking after your master, old girl – he *definitely* needs you!'

Wil turned towards the trees.

'Wil, wait!' Mortimer came crashing after him. He was waving something in his hand. 'You might need this.'

Mortimer held out the pink silk bag and smiled down at his friend. Wil looked at it and smiled back.

'No, Mortimer, you keep it – come by Mistlegard someday and cook some of that deer for my mother and I. Not too heavy on the juniper though!'

And, with an apologetic grin, Wil turned and walked away.

Standing under a thick pine tree, Wil listened as the others galloped off into the night. A lump stuck in his throat.

To his relief, Pricilla was waiting on the other side of the copse with Tinniswood's horse dozing next to her.

Actually getting back into the saddle was a bit easier, but making the horse move once again was proving to be much more difficult and for a moment Wil wondered if the horse was trying to tell him that he was doing the wrong thing; he could certainly tell that Pricilla was less than impressed, and Wil's own conscience had stopped speaking to him altogether!

'Look,' he said into the darkness, 'I've made up my mind. I'm going home and that's the end of it!'

Pricilla launched into the sky with a single beat of her wings and the horse moved off at a slow, steady walk.

'Thank you!' said Wil. He was tired and hungry, and the nagging feeling that he had let people down was making him bad-tempered. He had no idea of where he was going except that if the others had gone east, he needed to go north.

Crump![106]

Wil didn't know how long he had been asleep, but he did know that falling off that blessed horse – *yet again* – hurt!

He lay there in the dirt, with his cheek pressed into a muddy puddle. The horse stood over him, munching great clumps of grass. It was dawn – again. He had spent yet another night lost on the fells.

Staying right where he was, in the mud, he allowed himself a moment of bad language then, feeling no better, he got to his knees and shook the mud out of his hair.

'Crronk!'

Wil jumped. Pricilla was perched on the horse's saddle – and in her razor sharp beak was a small bag – but *not* the familiar pink silk one.

She fluttered down and dropped the bag at Wil's feet – a freshly baked loaf of bread rolled onto the grass. Wil picked it up. It was still warm and the smell of fresh baked yeast and malt made his mouth water. He ripped the end off the bread with his teeth and reached back into the bag. His fingers closed around a lump of cool waxy cheese; there was also a bright red apple, two pears and a flask of... elder wine.

He looked round, half-expecting to see Lady Élanor standing behind him. But no. He stopped chewing. He was right in front of the town gates of Saran.

'Wil, you're back!'

A small silver blur ran through the gathering crowd. Tally threw her arms around Wil and hugged him while a guard grabbed his arm.

'I... we've been so worried! Oh, Wil... Look Eli, it's Wil, he's back!' Lady Élanor's expression was much harder to read. After a quick glance towards Wil's cloak-covered shoulder, she looked into his eyes and then looked away without saying a word.

Confused by Lady Élanor's cool reception, Wil searched the crowd but there was no sign of Gisella, Mortimer or Seth. His heart sank.

'Tally, where are the others?'

'Becky, Emmet, Curtis, Leon and Olivia came back two days ago. They... they told us what happened to Giles. They said you went with Mortimer and Gisella. Aren't they with you, Wil?' Tally looked behind him as if she expected to see them standing there.

'No, er, we got split up – they, uh, left without me,' Wil answered – which, in one way, was actually the truth – they had gone without him!

'*They what!*' said Tally, but before she could interrogate him further another voice interrupted her.

'Well, well, Wil Calloway! After all that you've done, boy, I can't believe you've got the nerve to show your face!' It was Godwyn Savidge. 'Well at least *now* we'll get justice!'

'What do you mean, Godwyn?' Lady Élanor stepped in front of Wil but a crooked smile broke across the man's face. The guard tied Wil's hands behind his back.

'You may have managed to stall this young man's fate, my lady, but I am certain that it is because of him that my son met with such a terrible fate on Tel Harion!' Savidge paused, took a laboured breath and then continued. 'And now, finally, I can *absolutely prove* that he is guilty as charged of the attempted murder of Seth Tanner... This time, my Lady, there will be no delay; this time, there *will* be a hanging!'

The crowd cheered. Savidge gave the order to get the gallows ready.

'Take him to the Great Hall,' he shouted. 'Find Mortens and the others. I want this fiasco over by noon – *TODAY!*'

'Eli, do something! This isn't right!' Tally cried but the guard, with his chest puffed out with importance, pushed Lady Élanor aside, poked his sword sharply into Wil's back and drove him away across the square.

As he passed by, Lady Élanor grabbed hold of Wil's arm, 'You have trusted me up until now, Wil Calloway. Trust me *now*, I beg you!'

CHAPTER TWENTY-THREE

Questions, Questions

Once again Wil stood in the Great Hall. Once again the Order of the Magewizen of Saran took their seats[107] below the heads of three Wraithe Wolves – a lasting reminder of the night the Moon Chase went badly wrong – and once again the gallery was packed with people.

A door opened behind Wil. He span around hoping to see his friends. Annabel Prinze, the Order's Prosecutor walked in, and she was looking very pleased about something. Becky Lum, Olivia Drews, Leon Beck, Curtis Waller and Emmet MacPhee followed her; all five looked pale and tired. Olivia's eyes were red and swollen – she'd been crying again.

Wil watched the door, but Gisella, Mortimer nor Seth came in.

On the other side of the hall another door opened – they'd come! But no – it was Lady Élanor. The door slammed firmly behind her.

Olivia looked at Wil and started to sob loudly. Leon patted her shoulder and Miss Prinze gave her a handkerchief before showing Becky and the others to seats along the opposite wall. As Leon walked past he turned and spat in Wil's face, then he plonked down next to Becky and folded his arms tightly across his chest. The look he gave Wil was pure hatred.

Lady Élanor moved towards Wil but Godwyn Savidge jumped to his feet. Morten Mortens looked up in surprise as Savidge spoke.

'Master Calloway will *not* be requiring your services, Lady Élanor; we have already heard your argument *and* deliberated[108] on it.'

'Here, here!' Oswald Beck called in agreement. Fermina Fairfax was also nodding silently. But Agatha Peasgood shook her head; she did not look like she agreed at all.

'But Sir, Grand Wizen, your Worship,' said Lady Élanor, looking at Morten Mortens not at Godwyn Savage. 'If these five people have been brought here as witnesses, Master Calloway must be able to question them.'

'Well, um... Yes – that is what usually happens. Godwyn, I certainly can't think why...' the Grand Wizen began but Savidge, still on his feet, didn't let him finish.

'Well, I can! There is only one key question that needs to be asked and the answer will absolutely prove that Master Calloway is guilty!' His cheeks were puce[109] and his breathing was laboured[110].

Morten Mortens frowned.

'Well, perhaps,' he said carefully, 'we could hear the question and then have a vote on whether he can ask any, er, questions... Oh, and I haven't had any breakfast yet, so please excuse me if you hear my tummy rumbling.'

Wil closed his eyes – this was not going at all well.

'Miss Prinze – Annabel. Please read out the key question and tell us who will be answering it.' Morten Mortens gave the Prosecutor a cheerful smile.

But Wil already knew what the question would be – and he was certain who would be asked. He looked at the floor and waited.

'Yes, your Worships. Thank you,' beamed Miss Prinze. 'I intend to ask Becky Lum to tell us if she was aware of any injury that the accused incurred while he was on the Moon Chase three nights ago.'

She smiled at Becky. Becky did not smile back.

'As you know, your Worships,' Miss Prinze continued. 'The Order of the Magewizen of Saran has decreed[111] that the death of Wil Calloway *or* any injury during the recent Moon Chase, would confirm that he is guilty of the attempted murder of Seth Tanner. As you can see, your Worships, Master Calloway is alive. He is in this hall today. Master Tanner, however, is not.'

Wil leant forward. He was about to jump up and object when a familiar voice whispered in his head.

'W*ait, Wil – trust my sister!*'

Wil glanced up at the gallery. A small, pale girl with silver hair looked down at him through the palest blue eyes.

Morten Mortens nodded.

'Mm, yes, I was wondering about Master Tanner. Also, weren't Mortimer Merridown and Gisella Fairfax with Master Calloway... and two Fellhounds?'

Miss Prinze answered immediately.

'It appears that Seth Tanner, most likely still in shock from the attack, went to join the Moon Chase, your Worships. Master Calloway must have made a second, more successful attempt to kill Seth and then killed the others, too, your Worships.'

This was too much for Wil.

'No, that's wrong. I didn't kill them! *I DIDN'T KILL ANYONE!*' he shouted.

The Prosecutor looked at him, her eyebrows raised.

'That's a nasty temper, Master Calloway.'

The crowd in the gallery jeered.

'Get on with it!' someone shouted.

'Master Calloway, please could you refrain from further outbursts or this is going to take quite a long time,' said the Grand Wizen.

'*The longer the better!*' thought Wil, but he managed not to say it out loud.

'*Wil... please... just trust Élanor,*' Tally's voice whispered. Wil sat back down and held his head in his hands – he just wanted the nightmare to end.

'Right, well, now we've heard Miss Prinze's key question, are we going to vote on whether Master Calloway, or his representative, will be able to cross examine Becky Lum?' Morten Mortens gave an enthusiastic nod to the other members of the Order. 'All those in favour raise their hands.'

Both he and Agatha Peasgood put their right hands straight into the air. The other three wizens sat with their hands firmly in their laps. Mortens looked genuinely disappointed.

'Ah... and all those a–' Oswald, Savidge and Fairfax's hands were already in the air before he could finish. '–gainst? Oh dear... well, we did agree.' He smiled apologetically at Lady Élanor but avoided Wil's face all together.

'Well, Miss Prinze... please call your witness?'

Becky Lum stood in front of the Order. Her fingers were clasped together in front of her. Her face was pale.

'Miss Lum, thank you for coming here today. Do you understand the charges against this young man?' Miss Prinze pointed towards Wil.

Becky nodded. 'Yes, Ma'am,' she said quietly, not raising her eyes from the floor.

Olivia started sobbing again. The prosecutor spoke a little louder.

'Now Miss Lum, I am going to ask you a question and I ask that you answer it in as much detail as you can. Do you understand?'

Becky gave a tiny nod.

'For the court, then, Miss Lum, could you tell us if Master Calloway was injured during the Moon Chase?'

There was a long pause.

'Miss Lum? Do you understand the question?'

Becky looked very uncomfortable.

'Yes, Ma'am... yes, I... I believe he was injured – by a Wraithe Wolf... but not like Giles!' Becky answered.

'And where was he injured, Miss Lum?' asked Miss Prinze.

'In Skelmer Hollow – just after Giles was... you know... taken.'

Olivia sobbed uncontrollably. One of the guards rushed forward and guided the weeping girl from the hall.

'No, Miss Lum, I meant, where was he injured on his body?' said the Prosecutor patiently.

'Oh... his arm, I think – or his shoulder? It was dark – I couldn't see too well.'

'Was anyone else with you at this time?'

Becky gestured to Leon.

'Leon was there, but he got knocked out.'

'By Master Calloway?' asked Miss Prinze, her eyebrows once more forming high arches.

'No! Gosh, no. By a wolf, I think – I wasn't there then.'

'Was anyone else there?' pressed Miss Prinze.

'Yes – Gisella.'

'Gisella Fairfax, Wizen Fermina Fairfax's only child – who is now missing,' said the Prosecutor. Fermina Fairfax sat, white faced, but did not look up.

'Did you discuss Master Calloway's injury with Miss Fairfax?'

Lady Élanor walked forward, 'Grand Wizen, your Worship – I thought Miss Prinze was going to ask just one question?'

'No, no.' Fermina Fairfax spoke before the Grand Wizen had time to open his mouth. 'I distinctly heard Godwyn say one *key* question – I did not think that it would be the *only* question. Did you, Prosecutor?'

'Gosh, no, your Worship. To allow me only one question would have been absurd![112]'

Godwyn Savidge jumped to his feet again.

'With all due respect, Grand Wizen,' he said, not looking in the least bit respectful. 'Let's just get to what we already know. That is, that during the hunt this boy distracted my son, Giles, causing him to be attacked by a Wraithe Wolf. But Calloway suffered a blow to his shoulder. Becky saw the wound. Calloway's guilt was proved so he tried to escape. Seth Tanner, Mortimer Merridown and Gisella Fairfax tried to stop him and he killed them. Therefore, it's obvious – he must hang as the murderer he is!'

Godwyn banged his fist down on the table. Everyone in the gallery started cheering and shouting. Fermina Fairfax and Oswald Beck clapped. Agatha Peasgood went as white as a sheet and Morten Mortens looked utterly defeated[113].

Wil looked upwards – there had to be some way out of this nightmare. A movement at a tiny window high up near the rafters caught his eye. There, silhouetted against the bright morning light, was the shape of a large bird.

In the next second Lady Élanor was standing at Wil's side. The noise in the hall was deafening.

She shouted into his ear, 'Wil, take off your shirt!'

'What?'

'Take off your shirt… and the bandage. Quickly!'

The silence was immediate. Everyone in the hall stared. Wil was standing in the cold hall, naked to the waist – with not a mark on him.

'This cannot be,' breathed Godwyn Savidge. 'But she told us… that bandage…'

As he tried to understand what he was looking at another voice broke the shocked silence.

'That bandage, your Worship, was to protect his shoulder while he fired his bow.'

Wil's heart filled with joy. There in the gallery, large as life, stood Mortimer, Seth and Gisella. It was Gisella who had spoken out – loud and clear so that there was no mistaking what she had said. She continued.

'Becky and I were mistaken, your Worships. When we saw the blood all over Wil we did think he'd been injured. But it was wolf blood. Its heart had exploded under the impact of my bolt. Wil was just in the way and got covered. Then we were busy with Olivia and the dead wolves... and then we all got split up, so Becky never got to see what had really happened.'

'Yes, but he got my son killed!' Godwyn insisted.

'No, Sir. It was Giles's fault he was taken,' said Mortimer. He looked down at the red-faced man. 'It was Giles's fault, too, that he got injured before. He was so desperate to prove he should be a Chaser that he didn't care about anyone else.'

The people around Mortimer gasped.

'What nonsense is this?' blustered Godwyn. He turned to Leon, Emmet and the others for support but Mortimer would not stop.

'I was there, sir. I saw what he did with my own eyes. Wil did nothing. Giles made Olivia swap places with him – even though he knew that she can't use a crossbow. He left her to die, just like he left the others. If we hadn't had Wil Calloway with us that night, I doubt that any of us would have come off Tel Harion alive.'

Mortimer's words hung in the air. A few people coughed quietly and a small child started to whine. A ray of bright sunlight shone into the hall through one of the narrow windows. Wil could see particles of dust floating in the light. His skin started to prickle with cold.

'Somebody get that boy a cloak!' ordered the Grand Wizen suddenly. Lady Élanor folded Old Barrowman's cloak around Wil's shoulders and walked out of the hall.

A short while later, Wil stepped out into the morning sunshine – free at last. Godwyn Savidge had not said another word during the rest of the hearing; Oswald Beck had listened and nodded. Wil got the distinct impression that the Grand Wizen was happier to hear of Tinniswood's demise at Esk Falls and the location of the missing hinds than anything else. Fermina Fairfax, though, had started to behave very strangely and kept laughing at nothing.

Finally Morten Mortens cheerfully declared Wil innocent; the Moon Chase was held a success and

Giles's fate was accepted as one of the risks that Fellmen know they are taking when they joined the hunt. He then announced that he was going off to have a late breakfast and if anyone else was hungry they were welcome to join him.

Standing now in the town square, Wil let the fresh, autumn air fill his lungs. For the first time in days he felt he could actually breathe without a huge weight pressing down on his chest. Somewhere, someone was cooking bacon – it smelt fantastic!

'Wil, Eli says you're to come to the Hall before you go home,' called Tally as she sped towards him, beaming. 'Please say you'll stay another day! Please, please! Martha's baked a turkey and ham pie and the most wonderful smelling bramble pudding. And you should see the puppies – they've grown huge in the past week, you won't believe your eyes when you see them...'

She gabbled on, dragging him by the arm along the main street. Once again, people stopped to look up at him. But this time some waved, others smiled and one lady presented him with a shiny apple; girls pointed and giggled behind their hands and a group of boys tucked their hands deep into their pockets and nodded in sullen approval as he passed by.

The door to a small, run-down stone cottage creaked

open and an old man with a wart on his nose shuffled out. 'I thought you 'ad the makin's of a Fellman, boy!' he said to Wil. 'Yer mother'll be proud o' yer – make no mistake!'

CHAPTER TWENTY-FOUR

Lovage Hall Again

The second Tally opened the gate Wil heard the sound of giant claws scrabbling on gravel and a huge Fellhound bounded around the corner of the Hall. Her powerful tail whirled around as she greeted her friend.

'Farrow!' exclaimed Wil as the hound almost bowled him off his feet. She pushed her head into his shoulder and leant against him groaning with pleasure while he scratched her ear. Tally let go of Wil's arm and skipped into the house to announce his arrival.

Seth rounded the same corner and beamed.

'Oh, right! Well I can see where *her* loyalties lie!' Farrow bounded back to him and nuzzled his chin. 'Yes, I know, Farrow, I'm pretty pleased to see he's okay, too!'

Seth and Farrow led Wil around to the side garden. Gisella was sitting on a tree stump sipping a glass of Martha's sarsaparilla and burdock.

'So you decided to come back after all then?' she said without a smile.

'Uh, yeah,' answered Wil, suddenly feeling awkward. 'Well, actually the horse decided to bring me back!'

Gisella did not look impressed. Wil tried again.

'Anyway, I'm glad it did – although I was a bit worried back there. Where were you lot?'

'Gisella took her bandage off. You remember – that cut on her leg,' said Seth, pointing at Gisella's leg just in case there was any doubt about where it was. 'It was amazing – no scar or anything. Completely healed! So she said that we had to find you because you'd be okay, too. So we went to look for you.'

'So even when you knew that I'd been injured, you still didn't think I was guilty?' Wil asked before Seth could go on.

'After you did all that out there? After *I* nearly got you all killed? There's no way you were guilty of trying to murder anyone, Wil!'

'So if you knew I was innocent why didn't you just leave me to go home?' asked Wil.

'Because we knew you had to clear your name,' answered Seth simply.

'And because if we did we knew we'd never see you again,' said Gisella.

Lunch went on for most of the afternoon. Lady Élanor and Tally listened while the four friends talked about Wraithe Wolves and waterfalls, fishing and fighting. As they talked Martha served up dish after dish of delicious food – she seemed to have guessed that they hadn't eaten much out on the Fells.

'Oh, I nearly forgot, Wil,' said Mortimer polishing off[114] the last spoonful of bramble pudding straight from the serving bowl – apparently the only brambles worth cooking had to be picked with the dawn dew dripping off them! 'This *really* is yours and I don't think Lady Élanor will forgive you if you don't take it back!'

Mortimer pushed the pink silk bag across the table towards Wil.

'So it was useful then?' asked Tally waspishly. Her mood had changed since they had sat down to eat; but Wil was determined not to let her spoil his last few hours with his friends and hoped she would snap out of it. He reached over and took the bag.

'Oh, yeah, thanks. It was great – Tinniswood's face was a picture when he pulled out that juniper! And to think – Giles thought it was a wash bag and threw it away!' Wil said waving the little silk bag towards Gisella.

'I'd forgotten about that – how did you get it back?' said Gisella. She had had quite a few glasses of elder wine and her cheeks had gone quite pink!

'I, er, just went back to get it – before we all left for the Moon Chase,' answered Wil – he really wasn't sure how much they knew about Lady Élanor, or Pricilla. A glance at Lady Élanor confirmed that she was grateful he had not shared their secret.

Gisella looked thoughtful for a moment and then said, 'He really wasn't very nice, was he?'

'Who – Giles? Misguided and spoilt, I'd say!' said Mortimer. '*Although* – we will certainly miss his father's money on the Moon Chase!'

The thought of future Moon Chases hadn't occurred to Wil at all. He wondered how Mortimer would manage without a hound but decided it was probably best not to ask, especially as it was partly Seth's fault that Tarek had been killed; he was sure that Seth felt bad enough as it was.

They talked for a while longer and then Mortimer announced that he really should go home. It was only then that Seth remembered he hadn't actually been home to see his parents yet!

'I'll go, too,' said Gisella, although she didn't look like she wanted to leave.

'Oh, er... well... I could walk down with you later... if you want to stay a bit longer?' said Wil suddenly awkward.

Tally was looking even more miserable now. She'd sunk down into her chair and was concentrating on picking her nails.

'I'm going up to see Willow's pups. Do you want to come with me, Wil?'

She slid off her seat and headed for the kitchen.

'Er, no, I'd better stay with this lot, thanks Tally. Maybe I'll come up in a bit?'

'Suit yourself!'

The door banged as she left the room.

'So, when are you thinking of leaving then, Wil?' asked Mortimer. He didn't seem to have noticed Tally's silent strop. He was now scraping out the empty bramble pudding dish with his spoon. Martha gently prized it from him.

'I want to get going at first light. My poor mother, she probably thinks I'm dead by now!' said Wil.

'Hey, we could ride out to the forest with you?' said Mortimer. 'At least we can make sure you get *that* far!'

'Not until you've all had a proper breakfast!' called Martha from the kitchen.

Gisella and Seth didn't need any persuasion. Wil was delighted.

'That'd be great! But I've got no intention of *riding* anywhere. My legs haven't let me down yet.

Horses,' he wrinkled his nose. 'Not for me thanks; it's too high up and too far to fall!'

Tally didn't appear at breakfast next morning. Lady Élanor didn't mention her absent sister and Wil noticed that Martha had only laid breakfast places for four at the big table in the living room.

Mortimer and Gisella arrived together; Seth, breathless and looking crumpled arrived just as Martha was dishing up fried eggs and bacon.

'Goodness me, did the smell wake you up?' grinned Mortimer.

'Uh... sorry... my mother didn't call me,' said Seth, doing up his shirt. His hair was sticking up and his shirt was only half tucked into his trousers. 'She said I've had more than enough danger for a boy of my age!' He helped himself to a piece of buttered toast. 'Luckily Farrow caught a rabbit and woke me up to show me.'

'But, Seth, you're training to be a chaser!' said Gisella.

'Yer... well, that's my dad. He wants me to be a chaser. To be honest, I'd much rather be a bearer – I can shoot much better than I can ride!'

'Well you can certainly shoot, Seth Tanner, thank goodness!' agreed Mortimer with a grin. 'Why don't you just tell your father – surely he'd understand? Do you want me to have a word with him?'

'Gosh, no, please don't do that!'

'But Seth, you'd be a great bearer. And now that Giles is gone we're going to need to find someone new. You'd be perfect!' said Gisella. Wil silently agreed. Seth was small for his age and way too accident prone to be riding around carrying a spear!

'I know. But my father was so proud when I was picked to train as a chaser – I just can't let him down.'

For a few moments the only sounds to be heard were scraping cutlery on china and the rattle of tea cups.

Mortimer swallowed his last mouthful of bacon and broke the silence.

'So Wil, what are you going to do when you get home?'

Wil told them about his promise to mend his mother's leaking roof and about how he helped with the chores because his father had been taken by Rexmoore's men years before. Gisella looked shocked.

'Don't you want to find out what happened to him, Wil?' she asked, wide eyed. 'I mean – I know that my father's dead and that he died by falling into a vat of maple syrup – my mother always told me she knew he'd come to a sticky end. I don't think she liked him much; I was only a baby, so I can't remember him. Aren't you tempted to go and look for your father?'

'It's not that easy, Giz. And how would my mother cope if they took me as well? Anyway, we heard

228

that Rexmoore killed my father and four others as an example to everyone to make them pay their taxes.'

'That's terrible – I'm so sorry Wil.' Gisella put her knife and fork together on her empty plate and sat back. Her sad expression filled Wil with the desire to go over and give her a hug, but he didn't like to with the others there – they'd probably laugh at him anyway.

'Well, if you do decide to try to find your father, Wil, I'd be happy to join you,' said Mortimer raising his cup to his friend as he spoke.

'And me – as long as no one tells my mother!' said Seth. They all laughed and the conversation moved, thankfully, on to lighter things.

Peals of laughter echoed around the house while Wil went up to the bedroom to collect his few belongings. He pulled the bedcovers straight and looked around. Old Barrowman's cloak was hanging over the chair, clean and dry. He carefully placed the hunting knife on top of it.

'You can keep those, they were for you anyway,' said a sulky voice from the doorway. Tally was leaning on the door frame with her arms folded.

'Tally, why didn't you come for breakfast?' asked Wil. He was pleased to see her before he went, but cross that she was being so difficult.

'I was busy,' she answered, looking down at her feet.

'Well, I'm glad you're here now. It wouldn't have been right leaving without saying goodbye – after all you and Lady Élanor have done for me.'

'We didn't really do anything – we just showed you – you did it all yourself. You and your new friends!'

'But you're my friends too, you and Eli – I hope you always will be.'

'So... does that mean that you'll come back...?' Tally kept her eyes fixed[115] on the wooden floorboards.

'Of course I will! I'll come back to see everyone!'

As he finished speaking Tally burst into tears.

'Everyone? Not just me, then? Now that you've got the wonderful *Gisella*? Well, I hope you'll be happy with your new *girlfriend!*'

She ran down the corridor and off down the stairs.

'What *did* I say?'

'Don't worry, Wil. She'll be fine by the time you come back to see us,' Lady Élanor now stood in the doorway grinning. Downstairs the kitchen door slammed and the tiny panes of glass in the bedroom window rattled. 'You will come back and see us, won't you, Wil?'

'Without a doubt, my Lady. I owe you my life – one day, maybe I can repay you.'

'Disposing of Sir Jerad Tinniswood has repaid us ten-fold, Wil. But please, come back whenever you wish and stay as long as you want.'

CHAPTER TWENTY-FIVE

A Parting Gift

The journey to Mistle Forest was surprisingly quick. They had talked all the way and even though Mortimer tried to insist that Wil rode with him, Wil was determined to keep his feet firmly on the ground.

Mortimer had brought along a new Fellhound. His name was Apophinis. He was just twelve months old and had only recently started his Fellhound training. Apophinis trotted along beside Farrow, occasionally grabbing hold of her tail or her ear in his teeth. Farrow patiently put up with him.

Wil watched as the young hound sniffed at every clump of grass, every branch and even the horses' hooves.

Apophinis was already as tall as Farrow, but thinner and very leggy. Gisella said he looked like a gangly teenager who wasn't completely in control of his limbs.

Seth tried to show Wil how a Fellman would control his hound from his horse but Apophinis got in the way; Seth's horse jumped sideways to avoid treading on the young hound and Seth tumbled to the ground. He sat there squinting up into the sunshine while the others hooted with laughter.

'You're just lucky I didn't bring my crossbow!' he grinned.

'Gosh, yes – you might have shot yourself as you came off!' said Gisella, then she reined-in her horse: 'Well, if you and Wil are on the ground, we might as well join you down there – it's not far now anyway.'

They finished their journey on foot. Farrow happily ambled along beside Seth, while Apophinis entertained them by racing after rabbits. To no-one's surprise he didn't catch any – although that didn't seem to stop him trying!

By mid-morning the tree-lined edge of the ancient forest was clearly visible. Wil's heart grew heavy as they walked – he was desperate to get back to see his mother, but very sad to be leaving his friends. It would have been great to watch Mortimer training Apophinis and, he thought to himself, maybe he could have got to know Gisella a bit better.

'Well, Wil, I bet thatching[116] doesn't seem quite so exciting now, after the Moon Chase?' said Mortimer. Wil got the distinct impression Mortimer was making an effort to break the melancholy silence[117] that had fallen over them.

'What? After nearly being mauled, turned into a Wraithe Wolf, drowned, sold to Rexmoore, drowned again and hung! I can tell you, Mortimer – thatching at this moment sounds like the best thing in the world – even if it does mean I'll have to go up on a roof!'

'So you don't fancy coming back to join us as a Fellman then?'

'Tempting though the offer is... no!'

Wil was flattered that Mortimer had even joked about him becoming a Fellman. But the howl of the Wraithe Wolves still echoed in his dreams – he would definitely not be sorry if he never saw one of those creatures again!

'Oh well, you'll just have to train Apophinis to herd sheep then!' said Mortimer. He stopped abruptly and called the hound away from a particularly juicy pile of horse dung.

'What?' Wil looked from Mortimer to the hound. 'But he's yours. You're going to train him to replace Tarek.'

Gisella and Seth were smiling at Wil's confused expression.

'What Mortimer is trying to say, Wil, is that Apophinis isn't *his* new hound – he's yours!' said Gisella, scratching the young Fellhound's ear. He sat back on his haunches and pressed his head into her hand – Wil was sure he was smiling!

'I can't take him, Mortimer. He's yours – what will you do? *What would my mother say?'*

'Well, I can't speak for your mother, Wil, but honestly – Apophinis is for you. He's one of Tarek's sons. I'm having one of his daughters, Mia. So don't worry, I won't be without a hound of my own. It's just that I think you were meant to be a chaser, Wil. Up there, on Tel Harion... without you things really would have gone badly wrong – no thanks to Giles!' Mortimer added bitterly.

Wil knew there was no point refusing. He just hoped his mother would be so pleased to see him alive that she wouldn't mind that he'd brought a huge new friend with him!

'OK,' he said eventually, grinning at Mortimer, 'but I'm not promising anything about becoming a Fellman – chaser, bearer or anything else!'

Farrow let out a bark by way of agreement and Mortimer gave Wil a firm hug.

'Most of the stuff you'll work out, Wil, but there's one rule that you must not break – never exercise a Fellhound either in the hour before he eats, or the hour afterwards.'

'Why, what happens if you do? Do they turn into a toadstool or something,' Wil joked.

But Mortimer's expression was deadly serious.

'No, their gut twists, their stomach fills with air and they die in agony *very* quickly. Believe me, Wil, it's *really* bad.'

'Isn't there any cure?' asked Wil. Apophinis was poking about in the dung again.

'Well, some people say that if you can get the air out they *may* survive – but I wouldn't like to try it. I'd rather look after my hounds properly in the first place!'

'What about horse dung?' Wil asked as he watched Apophinis. 'Does *that* count as food?'

Mortimer laughed suddenly, 'No, for some reason that doesn't seem to upset them – which is a good job because they seem to like it – a lot!'

CHAPTER TWENTY-SIX

From Out of the Forest

They had talked for a long time at the edge of the forest. Mortimer had given Wil lots of tips on how to look after Apophinis properly and Seth had added a few more of his own.

Gisella had joined in but when Wil eventually announced that he really did have to go, her chin had begun to quiver. Mortimer had given her a brotherly hug but Wil just hadn't known what to do – so he hadn't done anything.

'Well, I'd better go. With any luck I'll be home in time for lunch. I can't believe I actually ran all the way here!' he had said lightly.

'Well, I'm glad you did!' said Seth, grinning at him. 'And, well, look. I know I haven't said it before, but I'm sorry about everything that happened after you tried to rescue me. I think my dad's a bit embarrassed, to tell you the truth. He'd never admit it though!'

'Hey, that's okay, Seth. Anyway, if I hadn't followed Farrow that morning, I'd never have met you lot – not that I want to go through the last few days *ever* again, of course!'

'Well, anyway – thanks, Wil,' Seth said and stepping forward to give Wil a brief, rather awkward hug; then he stepped back looking embarrassed.

After yet another bear-hug Mortimer let Wil go.

'I refuse to say goodbye, Wil Calloway, because I know we'll see you again – so get going and have a safe journey!'

Gisella looked at Wil. What he *wanted* to do was rush up, take her in his arms and promise that he would return as soon as he possibly could. What he *actually* did was slightly different.

'Right, well, goodbye then... and, er... thanks for all your help and, er... keep practicing with that crossbow.'

As he spoke he held his thumb up in what he hoped looked like a positive and encouraging gesture.

'Yer, thanks, I will and... good luck with your mother's roof – try not to fall off,' said Gisella. Then, desperately blinking back tears, she jumped back onto her horse. 'I'll see you back at Saran then,' she said to Mortimer and Seth. Then she kicked her horse into a gallop and headed towards the Fell without a backward glance.

'If you don't mind me saying Wil, I don't think that went as well as it could have!' Mortimer said, wrinkling his nose as he squinted into the sunlight to watch Gisella's horse kicking-up great clods of mud as it disappeared into the distance.

To Wil's surprise his mother took the news of Apophinis remarkably well, which he put down largely to her relief that he'd come home safe and well; although during the rather trying journey home  'Apophinis' had become *Phinn*; it was quicker and easier to shout!

Within a few hours Wil had managed to persuade one of the farmers to let Phinn sleep in a disused sheep fold behind Wil's house. It had a good fence and a stone shed that Phinn fitted into nicely – once Wil had adjusted the door height slightly – sheep were a lot lower to the ground than a Fellhound! In exchange, Wil agreed to use Phinn to protect the farmer's flock on the hills during lambing in the following spring.

That first evening he and his mother had sat in front of their cosy hearth and he had told her all about the mistaken arrest. He watered down[118] the story of the Moon Chase but didn't tell her anything about

Tinniswood, or Gisella. He didn't really know why, but it just felt like the right thing to do.

He did, however, describe Lovage Hall in detail. His mother was a keen gardener and she asked questions long into the night about what they grew and how they used the produce.

As they talked Wil's mind wandered back to Gisella's face, filled with disappointment, as they had parted. Not for the first time that day, Wil wished he could go back and do that bit again!

He sat now; perched right on the top of the newly covered roof, proudly admiring the layers of tightly-packed golden reeds. Below, he could see Phinn, sprawled full-length in the old sheep fold – fast asleep on a slowly melting snow drift.

He smiled and squinted towards Peachley Hills. Lambing would be starting any day now and he hoped that Phinn would help him to live up to his promise to protect the new arrivals. Unfortunately, to-date, Phinn had only shown a keen interest in *playing* with the sheep – an interest which, much to Phinn's obvious disappointment, was not shared by the sheep.

From the roof Wil could see the dense trees of Mistle Forest – dark green pine highlighted with the pale greens and pinks of newly sprouting oak, beech and chestnut. He wondered, as he often did, how Gisella and the others were getting along.

It had been two months since he had watched Gisella's horse gallop away – two long winter months of dark, cold nights, a lake's worth of rain and, in the last few weeks, heavier snow than he could remember in any other winter. Even now, in the warm spring sunshine, he could still see pockets of white here and there around the village and the peaks of the surrounding hills rising up behind East Lake still looked very wintry.

As he sat pondering that disastrous parting once again, rehearsing what he would say to Gisella if he ever saw her again – *if she ever spoke to him again that was* – he spotted a black dot above the forest. At first he thought it was a crow, but as it came closer he could see that it was much bigger than any crow. He narrowed his eyes to get a better look – it was flying slowly, flapping its huge wings in great elegant sweeps. Closer and closer it came then finally the bird dived down past the last of the trees and headed straight towards Mistlegard.

'Crronk, Crronk, Prruk!'

'Pricilla?' Wil muttered, not quite able to believe his eyes. The bird soared over his neighbours' roofs and plonked down next to him on the crisp new thatch.

'Crronk!' she said, cocking her head to one side before she took off again and headed back towards the forest.

'No, wait, Pricilla! Come back!'

Then, through the trees, another movement caught Wil's eye.

A figure on horseback charged out of the darkness, silver cloak billowing – long silver hair, like the horse's mane, flying in the wind. Pricilla was soaring in front of the horse – she was leading the rider.

'Lady Élanor!'

Wil really did fall off the roof this time. He tumbled from the top of the new thatch and landed right in the middle of a pile of spiky cuttings.

He was hastily dusting himself off when Lady Élanor's horse skidded to a clattering halt[119] in front of his mother's cottage.

'Lady Élanor – what's happened?' he asked, pulling a reed from inside his vest.

Her pale cheeks were porcelain white. Her normally pale blue eyes were bloodshot and underlined with dark shadows – she looked as though she hadn't slept for days.

'Oh, Wil, I'm sorry – I had to come – it's Tally – she's been taken!'

'What! What do you mean 'taken', Eli?'

'Kidnapped... and–,' she broke down. 'They've taken Tanith!'

'Kidnapped? How do you know?' asked Wil, remembering how often Tally disappeared for hours in a bad mood.

'Because they left this!'

She fumbled inside her cloak and handed him a piece of scruffy parchment. Wil read the words, written in dark red – he hoped it was ink, but feared that it probably wasn't. They read, *'Give up the legacy or I will make your precious sister tell me where it is!'*

'Have you got any idea who wrote this?' Wil asked.

'Well, as Tinniswood's gone I can only guess it was Lord Rexmoore... or Imelda, my aunt – Tally's aunt – our mother's sister. I think Tinniswood may have found out something before he died and got a message back to Rexmoore.'

'But why would this note come from Imelda?'

'Rexmoore's just her puppet. Oh, Wil, what am I going to do? Tally doesn't know where the legacy is!'

'I know – she told me.'

'There's one other thing, Wil,' her face was ash-grey now. 'Fermina Fairfax hasn't been seen for two days. Gisella is worried sick. We need to find her. We need to find them all! Wil, please, will you help us?'

Wil looked down at the frightened woman. She was normally so calm. He hadn't realised before just how alike she and Tally were – the same silver hair, the same high cheekbones – although her sister's eyes could somehow see right through you; she was also, a lot of the time, far more moody!

'I'll go and get Phinn. You'd better come with me while I explain to my mother why I've got to go away again!'

GLOSSARY
(WHAT THE LITTLE NUMBERS ARE FOR)

You can use this glossary to find words or phrases you find in the book that you don't understand. Just look for the number and you can discover what the word or phrase means and see other words you could use instead.

		What does it mean?	**Other words you could use**
1	wedge	: a triangle shape △	chunk
2	pricked her ears	: her ears twitched because she was listening carefully	suddenly she looked up, listening
3	sped	: run fast	ran very fast
4	quick as a flash	: something happening very, very quickly	quick as lightening
5	up to no good	: doing something wrong	doing something bad
6	Elder	: an important person in the village	council member
7	slaughterer	: person who kills the farm animals for the villagers to eat	-

		What does it mean?	Other words you could use
8	cackling	: a nasty laugh, not nice	with a cruel laugh
9	pranced	: moving with springing steps	danced
10	infirmary	: a hospital	hospital
11	braced	: got ready for something to happen	prepared
12	thunk	: **Made up word**: the sound made when Lady Élanor's fingers flick on the bars of the prison cells	knock
13	clattered	: a rattling noise	clacked
14	shabby	: untidy	scruffy
15	Magewizen	: **Made up word**: these are the people who make the laws in Saran and make sure people stick to them	the court council

		What does it mean?	Other words you could use
16	Prosecutor	: a person who works in a court	accuser
17	Grand Wizen	: **Made up word:** The Head of the Magewizen; the most important wizen	leader
18	stand trial	: when a person is accused of a crime they must go to a meeting called a trial where the crime is discussed and other people decide what is the truth	be judged
19	witness	: a person who saw what happened	testifier
20	dabbed	: pat with your hand	patted
21	wizen	: **Made up word:** a person who is a member of the Magewizen	council member

		What does it mean?	Other words you could use
22	'All rise'	: When someone says "All rise" in a court everyone must stand up to show respect	'Everyone get up'
23	verdict	: the decision made by the court	decision
24	thatched	: a roof made of straw	-
25	foraging	: looking for food	search
26	pungent	: a strong smell	strong
27	innocent	: you have done nothing wrong	not guilty
28	reared up	: stood on its hind legs	jumped up
29	in a blink	: very quickly	in a trice
30	rickety	: something that might break at any moment	shaky
31	defend	: protect	stand up for

		What does it mean?	Other words you could use
32	fought the desire	: tried to stop himself doing something	resisted
33	barbarians	: cruel or brutal people	ruthless people
34	legacy	: when a person dies they sometimes leave money or property to someone else	inheritance
35	debate	: a discussion	argument
36	CLANNGGG!	: a very loud noise	DONG!!
37	peered	: looked at	squinted at
38	stride	: walk confidently	walk
39	back-patting	: patting someone on the back	friendly back slapping
40	hearty hugging	: giving someone a big cuddle	cheerful greeting
41	waspish	: annoyed	ratty
42	heart sank	: felt disappointed	hopes fell

		What does it mean?	Other words you could use
43	mounted	: got on their horses	climbed onto
44	reined-in	: stopped the horse by pulling on the reins	stopped
45	try as he might	: he tried really hard but couldn't do it	tried as hard as he could
46	I clean forgot	: I completely forgot	it slipped my mind completely
47	retched	: was nearly sick	gag
48	uncontrollably	: unable to stop	couldn't stop
49	burned	: was so painful it felt very hot	was very hot
50	hackles	: the fur, or hair, along the animal's back	hair
51	in the process	: while something is happening	at the same time
52	gnashing	: clashing teeth	snapping and growling

		What does it mean?	Other words you could use
53	acrid stench	: really horrible smell	pong
54	haunches	: back legs of an animal	rear legs
55	scrabbling	: trying to run but slipping and sliding	clawing
56	excruciating	: very bad pain	extremely painful
57	searing	: so painful it feels like it's burning	burning
58	waned	: gone away	disappeared
59	copse	: a clump of trees not big enough to be a proper wood or a forest	small wood
60	lame	: can't walk properly possibly because of an injury	limping
61	resist	: put up a fight	fight back
62	pushed on	: kept going	kept going

		What does it mean?	Other words you could use
63	engulfed	: completely covered over	consumed
64	gore	: blood and guts	blood
65	vomited	: was sick	threw up
66	trophies	: prizes	memento
67	seething anger	: really, really angry	rage
68	frantically	: really quickly, almost panicking	hurriedly
69	slain	: killed	dead
70	backed-up	: moved backwards without turning around	retreated
71	lone	: on its own	single
72	fascinated	: very interested	engrossed
73	combat	: fighting	battle
74	felled	: dropped (cut down like a tree)	killed
75	writhing	: wriggling in pain	squirming

		What does it mean?	Other words you could use
76	thwacked	: hit	stabbed
77	hurtled	: ran very fast	pelted
78	bowled me over	: knocked me down	knocked me down
79	horrendous	: really bad	appalling
80	plunged	: fell into	plummeted
81	admiration	: impressed	wonder
82	wander	: walk slowly	walk
83	dilute	: make weaker	wash away
84	erupting	: growing really quickly	coming through
85	burrowing	: tunnelling	cutting through
86	blustered	: talked quickly to get out of trouble	talked nervously
87	rainbow slick	: oil floating on water	colourful emulsion
88	out-voted	: everyone else wanted something different	out numbered

		What does it mean?	Other words you could use
89	tucking into	: eating hungrily	devouring
90	trudged	: walk with heavy footsteps	stomped
91	thuggish-looking	: rough, not nice	rough
92	rustling	: taking animals such as deer, sheep or cattle	stealing
93	tantalisingly	: making you want some	temptingly
94	chomping	: chewing loudly	eating
95	soothed	: talking calmly to make others feel calm	mollify
96	reverse side	: the other side	the back
97	emerged	: came out	appeared
98	milky darkness	: the fog made the darkness so cloudy they couldn't see through it	foggy night

		What does it mean?	**Other words you could use**
99	he reasoned	: he thought about the problem and came up with a solution	he thought
100	torrent	: fast flowing river	rapids
101	I'll pass	: I won't do it	I'll say no
102	swooped	: flew down quickly	dived
103	takin' you	: We are going to take you (a way of speaking)	taking you
104	crescents	: describes the moon when it is not a full moon – a 'crescent' is the name for the shape	sickle moons
105	I'd fight your corner	: I'd fight with you	I'd stand by you
106	Crump!	: **Made up word:** the sound of someone falling off a horse into thick mud	Thud!

	What does it mean?	Other words you could use
[107] took their seats	: sat down in their seats	sat down
[108] deliberated	: talked about	considered and discussed
[109] puce	: very red	bright red
[110] laboured	: something is hard to do	struggling
[111] decreed	: announced as the truth	decided
[112] absurd	: silly	ridiculous
[113] defeated	: beaten	beaten
[114] polishing off	: Finishing every bit	devoured
[115] fixed	: staring at	stared
[116] thatching	: making a roof out of straw or reeds	-
[117] melancholy silence	: no-one is talking because they are all sad	sad quiet

	What does it mean?	Other words you could use
[118] watered down	: missed some bits out so that it didn't sound so bad	dilute
[119] clattering halt	: the noise the horse's hooves made on the ground when Lady Élanor stopped her horse	noisy stop

Special thanks to:

my wonderful husband, Tim, who's faith keeps me going; Zein Pereira, whose expertise and patience are never ending; Ali Harries, for keeping my feet on the ground; Sam Wall and Alan Marks, for putting my thoughts into wonderful pictures; Big Jem, for making sure the words make sense and Ritchie Craven, for making it all real. Thanks also to the newest member of the family, Mojo, who came along at a time of need and filled a very big gap left by my beloved Finn – the inspiration goes on.